Heir of the Forgotten Realm

Heir of the Forgotten Realm

by
Michael J. Svigel

BAKER TRITTIN PRESS
Winona Lake, Indiana

Heir of the Forgotten Realm
By Michael J. Svigel

Printed in the United States of America
Cover Art: Paul S. Trittin

Published by Baker Trittin Press
P.O. Box 277
Winona Lake, Indiana 46590

To order additional copies please call (888) 741-4386
or email info@btconcepts.com
http://www.bakertrittinpress.com

Publishers Cataloging-Publication Data
Michael J. Svigel - 1973-
      Heir of the Forgotten Realm - Tweener Press Fantasy Series
      / Michael J. Svigel - Winona Lake, Indiana /
      Baker Trittin Press, 2006

        p.   cm.

Library of Congress Control Number: 2006934170
ISBN 10: 0-9787316-3-8
ISBN 13: 978-0-9787316-3-2
      1. Juvenile   2. Fiction   3. Fantasy
      I. Title   II. Heir of the Forgotten Realm
JUV037000

For Stephanie

Steps of the Journey

Acknowledgements

Books never write themselves, and authors never work in a vacuum. Though I often joke that I wrote *Heir of the Forgotten Realm* by accident, several people contributed to its birth and growth at various stages. I would like to especially thank the following:

Those who slogged or slashed through early drafts and provided helpful (and even unintentional) feedback: Scott Bean, Zach Bean, Meredith Burke, John Craig, Les Fleetwood, David Gregory, Jim Moore, and Alexander Wilhelm.

Dave Carl, creator of *Paws & Tales*, who helped me uncover the bigger story.

Brie Engeler, who pruned and polished the first draft with an eager and sacrificial heart.

Dr. Marvin Baker and Paul Trittin of Baker Trittin Press, whose noble and adventurous vision continues to turn wooden puppets into real boys.

My beloved wife, Stephanie, whose love and support in both life and work have always inspired me to do more than any man can realistically accomplish.

My precious children, Sophie and Lucas, whose enthusiasm for my bed-time "epics" drove the story night after night.

And, above all, the great Storyteller—whose truth dispels myth and whose epic defies legend.

Michael J. Svigel

Chapter One

Trallia

I

Little Lukas stood trembling in the center of a burning hallway as dancing flames and thick, black smoke closed in around him. His father, still dressed in his silk night clothes, held a sword in the air.

His mother's frantic voice cried out over the roaring fire, "Jon! Drop your sword and save our son!"

Suddenly his father stood over him. Tossing the sword aside, he reached down and snatched the little boy in his arms, rescuing him from the fire and heat.

Lukas could hear his father's pounding heart as his ear pressed against his chest. Shielding Lukas's head from the flames, his father ran down the hall until an explosion rocked the building. His mother screamed. His father stumbled.

Lukas fell.

He continued to fall through flame and smoke. As total darkness engulfed him, the faces of his mother and father receded into nothingness.

Lukas landed in his own soft bed. He was covered in sweat with his heartbeat thumping loudly in his ears. His own scream had awakened him, yet it was not the expected scream of a child but the scream of a man.

A palace guard slipped into the room. "Are you well, my lord?"

Lukas closed his eyes as the flames of his nightmare dissolved. "I'm fine, Taro . . . just a bad dream."

Taro shook his head. "Again? Miss Poppit's tea obviously didn't help."

"Like most of Miss Poppit's '*cures*' it seems to have made me worse," Lukas quipped.

His friend sat down in a chair just a few feet from the bed. "Should I light the torch?"

"No," Lukas answered much too quickly. "I . . . that's not necessary really. Thank you."

Taro sighed. "We've known each other all our lives, Lukas, and your fear of a flame has only grown worse."

Lukas's eyes rolled away from Taro, and he joked, "Maybe all of our years of friendship have made it worse."

Taro laughed. "No, my influence on you has been as bad as any of the servants and soldiers in Trallia but not to that end. For that you can blame a cook . . . or the blacksmith."

"You forget. I avoid those men like a mule avoids the whip."

"An apt analogy! Though I've never figured out what destiny has in store for you, I know you'll never be a blacksmith or a cook."

"Or a candle-maker," Lukas added.

"No, you could *make* them; you just couldn't *light* them," Taro shot back, standing up with a sigh.

"Your list of available occupations is far too short. I need to consider my options."

Taro shook his head. "You *still* don't know what you want to be when you grow up?" he asked sarcastically. "Well, thank goodness you don't have to make that choice yourself. Destiny's chosen it for you." He looked at his friend lying in the bed and shook his head again. "Get some sleep, and I'll be at my post with a washbowl ready to put out any fires . . . even the ones that are all in your mind." He reached for the chamber door to leave.

Lukas called through the darkness again, this time his voice suddenly serious: "Taro . . . thank you."

"My duty, m'lord," his friend replied with exaggerated salutes.

"No," Lukas insisted, "I'm serious. When I was brought here fifteen years ago, you became my friend at the start. You are like the brother I never had."

Taro nodded. "We'll be brothers again tomorrow, my friend, but tonight I'm posted as your guard. So get some sleep. You have a big day tomorrow, and you'll need more courage than you can imagine."

II

King Lundin observed the Spring Festival from his throne in the ballroom as his guests sang, danced, and laughed in concert with the lively music. Lords and commoners alike mingled on the palace grounds and the doors to the main ballroom stood open to allow anyone from the Kingdom of Trallia to come and go at will.

The king himself looked on with pride as his only daughter, Lilia, danced with Lukas. For the last few years, as Lukas and Lilia matured into young adults, whispers of their budding love had spread throughout the palace like the ivy vines growing on the castle walls. Only one week earlier when he celebrated his nineteenth birthday, Lukas had asked King Lundin for permission to marry his daughter.

The king had hesitated. "Though you're of noble blood, I wonder whether you're prepared to help Lilia rule Trallia after I'm gone." His voice slowed with uncertainty.

"I am," Lukas answered, and his own voice cracked with doubt. Deep inside, Lukas knew he had not been groomed for a life of politics, not of the sort that the kingdom would require. Through his marriage to Lilia he would gain not only the woman he loved but also responsibilities of state. It was a task he dreaded but one he believed he could face with Lilia at his side.

The king paused and pondered Lukas' answer. After some time he finally breathed out a long sigh and said, "You are a good man, Lukas. I have watched you grow up, treating you more like a son than a guest. You have much to learn, but you will have many opportunities to prove your worth." After a moment of silence he continued, "I have seen that Lilia looks upon you with great love, and because I look on her with the heart of a father and not of a king, I grant permission for you to marry." Then leaning forward in his seat, the king shook his finger and said slowly, "Do not disappoint me."

Rumors began to spread as soon as the king gave his blessing. Now, on the first day of the Spring Festival, all knights and knaves knew that it would not be long before Lukas asked for Lilia's hand in marriage.

Lukas and Lilia waltzed through the great ballroom doors out to the main garden courtyard with Lilia's delicate white dress swirling around their feet at every turn. She wore green ivy in her dark hair, matching the green tunic Lukas wore in the tradition of his native House of Stanton. When the music ceased and the crowd cheered, Lukas held Lilia's hand high as she bent forward in a slight bow. Lukas bowed as well, smiling lovingly into Lilia's dark brown eyes. With his right hand he gently touched her smooth cheek, and Lilia's shy gaze retreated to the marble pavement.

Then Lukas's own bow lowered to the ground as he dropped to one knee and gazed up into Lilia's eyes. The crowd grew quiet, and a moment later King Lundin himself joined the throng in the garden courtyard. Lukas held both of Lilia's hands in his firm but trembling grip.

The king looked on with apprehension wondering, *what would her mother say if she were alive to see this day?*

With all ears listening intently and all eyes watching carefully, Lukas nervously recited the words he had memorized. "Princess Lilia, today I give you my heart and swear before all the Kingdom of Trallia that I'll never take the hand of another in dance. You alone are the desire of my heart . . . and I love you." Lilia had fixed her gaze onto his bright, blue eyes. She dared not look away. After a long pause Lukas finally said, "Though I'm a lord without a land, the ward of servants and servant of lords, though I'm all these things and even less, will you, my dear princess . . . marry me?"

With those words Lukas reached into his vest pocket and removed a silver-chained necklace which held a brilliant red jewel carved into a perfect medallion, the traditional ornament worn by a betrothed bride of Trallia.

The crowd began to murmur as a wide smile shone on Lilia's face. She tentatively glanced at her father. He nodded in return. With tears of joy in her eyes she reached down and touched Lukas's shoulder. "Of course I'll marry you," she said softly.

The vast throng cheered and festive music burst forth. Without hesitation Lukas leapt to his feet and reached over Lilia's shoulders to clasp the necklace around her neck.

Shaking with nervousness Lukas struggled to attach the silver chain. As the trembling increased, Lukas realized that it had moved beyond his own hands. A deep rumbling that seemed to begin in his heart moved throughout his body and spread to the stone pavement. Quickly Lukas saw that everything around him was shuddering.

"It's an earthquake!" shrieked a frightened woman. Shouts and screams rippled through the crowd as people began running in every direction. The quaking intensified.

The necklace slipped from Lukas's light grip and landed on the marble with a hollow clink. Lilia and Lukas were staring at the floor when they heard the word that turned panic into pandemonium.

"Dragon!"

III

Lilia and Lukas turned their eyes toward the sky and saw a wingless, yellow serpent slithering through the air. It searched the ground intently, flying to and fro, its six eyes scanning the crowds. Each twist and turn of its giant snake-like body sent tremors of power echoing through the earth. With a sudden high-pitched roar and a red-hot blast of flames from its nostrils, the dragon turned its dark gaze directly on Lilia and dove toward her.

"Guards, draw your swords!" King Lundin shouted, trying to control the horror in his voice. Taro and two other soldiers stepped forward on command and readied themselves for battle, though they were unsure of how they could wage war against a serpent with twenty slithering, centipede-like arms.

Taro shouted at Lukas who stood with Lilia in the center of the courtyard: "Lukas, get Lilia into the palace!" Lukas looked at his friend but could not comprehend his words. He was like a statue, frozen in fright.

"Archers, fire at will!" the king yelled though his voice carried less confidence than his next command. "Everyone run for cover!"

A dozen archers immediately launched their arrows at the beast, but each weapon shattered harmlessly against the dragon's scales. Then with an angry blast of hot, putrid air from its snout, the dragon decimated the squad of archers. Men, women, and children alike covered their ears as the dragon let out a deafening roar. It passed overhead, hurled flames at the nearby village, and flattened buildings near the stables. Windows shattered while sections of the palace toppled.

Lilia and Lukas, knocked to the ground by the blast, struggled to climb to their feet. But the air around them was soon filled with fire and smoke. Swords melted, helmets and armor glowed red, and Lukas watched, horrified, as Taro turned to ash.

As the last blast of fire dissipated, panic replaced Lukas's shock. Images of fire and heat flashed through his mind. Lilia was screaming something at him, but all he heard was his own heart pounding and the dragon thundering as it writhed in the air and turned back for another pass. Looking over Lilia's head Lukas saw the dragon move straight toward them, smoke rising from its nostrils. Though his head and his heart told him to protect the princess at any cost, his fear of the dragon's flames overpowered his will, and he turned to flee. Abandoning Lilia to whatever fate may come, Lukas dove for safety from the dragon's fiery breath.

While he buried his head in his arms and screamed in mental torment, Lukas heard a loud thud, a muffled scream, and a final violent quaking as the dragon swooped back into the sky. The attack was over as abruptly as it had begun. The dragon's roar ceased. The tremors subsided. The screams of the festival guests turned into moans and laments.

Then King Lundin's shout was heard above the whimpering crowd: "Lilia! She kidnapped Lilia!"

IV

With soot in his golden hair and the taste of smoke and ash on his lips, Lukas clambered to his feet and peered into the sky with burning eyes. The yellow dragon flew toward the clouds holding Lilia firmly in one of its twenty claws.

Silently King Lundin stooped to grab the silver necklace that had fallen to the ground. Without a word, he roughly thrust it into Lukas's hand and looked back into the clouds in disbelief. "She needed you, lad," the king whispered through clenched teeth, "not your heart, not your hand. She needed your courage . . . but you fled."

"The . . . fire . . ." Lukas stammered. He turned away from the king in shame and stared at the pile of dust that was once his friend, Taro. Tears welled up in his eyes and rolled down his cheeks. He fell to the ground, cradling his head in despair.

The king's voice turned from disappointment to regret. "I know you fear fire as wicked men fear death. I knew you would fail, lad. You will always be the same. Your fear binds you with unbreakable chains." With those words the king started toward the palace, ignoring the moans and cries of the injured around him.

Lukas closed his eyes and fought against the memories smoldering deep inside his mind. They had singed his midnight dreams for years; he would not let them ignite his waking hours. Looking back to the king, he called out, "Please, my lord, give me charge of a hundred men, and I'll leave before the beast is out of sight! The flames of hell itself won't stop me again!"

"No, lad," the king snapped without turning. "Not even a thousand men can defeat *that* creature."

Confusion replaced Lukas' urgency. "What do you mean?"

"Follow me," the king said, "and I'll show you."

King Lundin led Lukas deep below the castle to a secret study lined with ancient books and scrolls. It was a chamber Lukas had never discovered in all his boyhood years of exploring the castle. In the center of the dim room sat a small table with a tiny wooden chest carefully placed on top. The king opened it with a creak. "Her name is Haarlok," he said, "the mother of the dragons. She's the last and worst of her kind. She's from that forgotten realm between myth and reality, legend and history . . . like the world that once was before wise men replaced poetry with prose, before heroes exchanged swords for words; and before the extinction of virtuous men. The dragon Haarlok is virtually invincible. No mortal weapon can harm her. No mere knight, however brave, can defeat her."

Lukas dropped into one of several rickety reading chairs and put his head in his hands. "Then I will die trying," he moaned.

"That's probably true," the king said, turning to Lukas with a tattered scrap of parchment in his hands, "but legends exist that speak of one way to defeat that rotten, yellow beast. They will sound strange and fantastic. You will want to doubt my words, but they represent our only hope." He handed the parchment to Lukas. "This is the first piece of a fourfold map. This section reveals a hidden path to the secret Valley of Validaan which is two days' journey to the northwest. The geography should be familiar enough to you if you kept up with your studies. The walled garden holds not only the second part of the map, but also the famed Helmet of Validaan, the first of four powerful weapons necessary for defeating the dragon. The other weapons you must seek are the Sword of Sapentia, the Armor of Fortis, and the Shield of Aequant. All four are essential in order to defeat this foe. She cannot stand against them."

V

Scanning the map fragment, Lukas noticed some strange symbols along the bottom edge.

"What are these markings? I don't recognize them. I don't know this language."

"It's an ancient dialect of the dwarves. The first word is *kogah,* 'power' or 'strength.' It's part of a message that can only be completed by the other three fragments. The message will reveal how to use the weapons against the dragon."

"How do you know this?" Lukas finally asked.

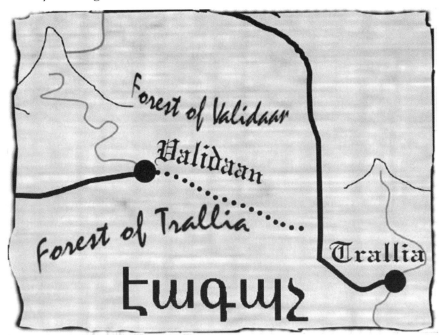

For a moment King Lundin appeared to look away in shame. Stumbling over his words, he said, "That . . . story will require too much time. I believe that the dragon took Lilia because she is my only daughter and heir to the throne. The Trallian kings of old slew the dragon's children and consorts, and she has returned to exact her revenge. She expects me to pursue her, but I cannot do so for reasons that may not be revealed." Staring through Lukas with piercing brown eyes, King Lundin clasped Lukas's shoulders and said, "Do not fail again, lad. Lilia's life and Trallia's hope are in your hands."

Lukas swallowed hard. Many more questions rushed through his mind, but the image of the yellow serpent escaping with Lilia called him to haste. He slid the map into his pocket and announced, "I am leaving right away, my lord. I shall find these four weapons and return with your daughter . . . or I will not return at all."

The king's voice lowered to a whisper, and his eyes narrowed to slits. "Beware of the Valley of Validaan. The region is cursed with dark desire and men have become mad with hunger, lust, and greed. Those who stumble into its deep ravines rarely return, and those who escape are never the same again."

"Yes, my lord," Lukas answered. He turned to leave, but the king called to him once again.

"Lukas, my lad, there are scores of men both noble and base seeking these same four weapons. You must succeed where others have failed and make great haste before any other man succeeds. For they have no interest in valor, wisdom, courage, or justice. They care nothing for defeating Haarlok or restoring security. They seek these weapons only as treasures for their own kingdoms and their own personal glory."

"But my lord," Lukas answered, "I am seeking only one treasure and neither will a thousand flaming dragons nor vain warriors keep me from Lilia."

As Lukas rushed from the secret room, the king sighed heavily and nodded. "He loves her indeed, perhaps too much. He cannot fathom what lays ahead, dangers no man has been able to overcome for centuries . . . not even I." With those words King Lundin opened the wooden chest again and stared in shame at a large apple of solid gold. Closing his eyes, he said, "Let him not make the same mistake as I."

Chapter Two

The Garden of Validaan

I

When Lukas reached the point of entry into the dense forest of Validaan, his horse could no longer continue. Lukas dismounted and left the animal to graze along the road as he began the difficult trek northwest. He followed a faint, overgrown path as it descended into the Valley of Validaan. Late in the night when his body grew weary and his eyes became heavy, he started a small fire and slept in the chill of the forest, expecting to move well and quickly the next morning. However throughout the night he dreamed of fire and awoke well before dawn, unable to return to sleep.

As he gathered his belongings, Lukas discovered that his sack of food had been ripped open and dragged away; its contents were devoured by animals in the night. Frustrated and confused, Lukas continued on, trudging alone through the thick forest.

The farther he penetrated the forest of Validaan the stranger it became. In some places the massive trees appeared frozen in the throes of battle as they viciously contended for the sparse light of the sun. In other places gangly trunks with bristling branches stood in long rows like soldiers assembled for war. It was impossible to tell where one tree stopped and the next began. Only with great effort could Lukas discern the untidy route coiling along the forest floor. At times he had to hack through branches with his short, steel blade or climb over trees that had fallen across the trail. When his sword finally shattered under the strain, Lukas discarded it and wrestled his way through the forest with his bare hands.

By the middle of the second day the path descended into a deep ravine. Without warning Lukas stumbled from the dense woods and found himself facing the massive eastern wall of the Garden of Validaan. The colossal stone barrier appeared to be barely holding back the crooked edge of the forest from encroaching into its territory — two opponents engaged in an ancient battle, neither side wanting to make the first move.

A tangle of thorn-studded vines covered the three-story wall rendering it impossible to climb. Lukas followed the wall for almost a quarter of a mile before reaching the southeast corner. He stopped to rest. With no food for over a day his stomach growled with a fierce hunger. After a few minutes in the cool shade, he returned to his feet and followed the wall west for another quarter of a mile until he reached the massive gate of Validaan.

The gate — wrought iron bars twisted into an ornate work of art — was twice Lukas's height and five times his width. He could see through the gate into the Garden of Validaan, and even this partially-obscured view made his heart leap and stop at the same moment. Captivated by the sight, Lukas failed to notice the enormous snake as it descended from above the gate until it hissed with its forked tongue just inches from his face.

Lukas jumped back with a start as the snake gracefully slithered through the gate and spoke in a deep yet strangely toneless voice: "Welcome to Validaan, young traveler."

Lukas eyed the snake suspiciously as it slinked through the iron bars of the gate and twisted again to speak to him. "I suppose you want to pass," it hissed.

"Yes . . . er . . . sir, I do." Lukas had never seen or heard a talking snake before, and for a moment he thought he might be dreaming.

"And I suppose you're seeking the Helmet of Validaan like the rest."

Lukas slowly nodded.

"Nobody comes for the serenity or beauty of the garden anymore. Men no longer seek the waters that reflect the unknown future or portray what might have been. They are all looking for the Helmet, but none have found it. Nevertheless entrance into the Garden of Validaan is still free," the serpent said, "and the Helmet sits unguarded at the end of the path." Pausing, the snake pulled apart the iron latch, and the gate slowly creaked open.

"Thank you . . . sir," Lukas said as he took a cautious step toward the gate.

The serpent's head suddenly dropped again, stopping Lukas in his tracks.

"Entrance is free, but you must follow one Law," the snake explained. "You must swear an oath that you will not remove anything from the garden, neither plant nor herb, water nor rock. You must not eat of any fruit or pluck any flower. *Swear it.*"

Lukas hesitated. His empty stomach protested, but he had set his heart and mind on Princess Lilia. He desperately needed to find the Helmet. "I swear it," he said.

"Then enter the Paradise of Validaan," the snake responded, slowly receding into the vines that covered the wall.

Lukas paused and then tentatively began to walk along the garden path as the iron gate locked behind him.

The path wound through lush trees and plants Lukas had never seen before. Bouquets of flowers grew in enormous beds where he could have comfortably slept. Colorful birds and butterflies gathered succulent nectar from the blossoms while a potpourri of sweet-smelling aromas filled the air. Playful brooks accompanied chirping birds and crickets, and a cool mist wafted across the rich, dark soil and dense, green grass. Every few steps full trees offered luscious, ripe fruits or fist-sized nuts, tempting travelers on the path. Lukas wanted to pluck them from the branches and fill his empty stomach, but he resisted the urge with every ounce of his will.

II

After walking along the path for nearly half an hour, the garden opened into a massive orchard where the way veered sharply to the north. Every tree in the grove grew to exactly the same average height, and the grove appeared to go on forever. As he peered into its depths, Lukas realized that many people moved slowly beneath the shadowy boughs, climbed into the branches and plucked fruit from among the green leaves. *Don't they know the Law?* Lukas wondered.

Then Lukas noticed several groups of men and women seated in the orchard talking, laughing, singing, and eating. His mouth began to water, and his body felt twice as exhausted and famished as it had a moment earlier.

Without warning a short, plump man with a long beard and ragged clothes stepped from the orchard and spoke to Lukas in a booming voice, startling several birds that darted from a nearby tree. "Try this one, lad," he said. In his hand was a luscious red fruit.

"No, thank you," Lukas answered, taking a step back.

The man persisted: "Take it! It's sweeter than honey. You've never tasted anything like it!"

Lukas saw rich, thick juice oozing from the fruit's center. His curious eyes were drawn to several of the other trees, and he quickly realized that they were teeming with the strangest fruits and nuts imaginable: large, candied almonds; overgrown apples, oranges, pears, and giant berries glistening in beads of dew.

The fat man smiled, "There are thousands more deeper in the grove. Try one." He offered Lukas the fruit again.

Lukas lifted the fruit from the man's hand. Immediately the sticky juice ran down his hand and his mouth began to water. *Maybe just one bite would tide me over,* he thought. *Besides, the serpent said I couldn't* eat *the fruit. He didn't say I couldn't* taste *it.*

As he wondered whether or not he should just take a nibble, he looked closely at the people sitting under the trees. Everyone had filled their laps with fruits and nuts as well as other things that looked like pastries and cakes. Their clothes fit too tightly — if they fit at all — and were stained with sauces, frostings, juices, and fillings. Every person's teeth were loose, stained, rotten, or simply missing. By the looks of them the orchard dwellers had been gorging on the fat of the land for a long, long time.

Lukas handed the fruit back to the fat man who suddenly frowned.

"No, thank you," Lukas said, "I promised that I would not eat anything."

The man stared at Lukas for a moment, squinted his eyes, and then broke his suspicious silence with loud laughter. Suddenly the rest of the orchard dwellers joined in, pointing their fingers at Lukas, and eventually rolling on the ground in raucous laughter. "He promised!" they teased. "The good boy promised!"

Ignoring them, Lukas turned and continued down the garden path with their hideous cackling still ringing in his ears and his hollow stomach urging him to reconsider.

Within a few yards the path crossed a wide, slow-moving stream. Lukas leaned over the low wall of the bridge and rinsed the juice from his fingers. As he stared into the glassy surface of the magical waters, his reflection was suddenly replaced by a vision of what might have been. He saw himself sitting with the others in the orchard. Fat, grubby, and out of control, his mouth was stuffed with all sorts of sweets.

Lukas shook the vision from his mind and rose to his feet. The image dissolved, and he stared once again at his own frightened reflection. As a little boy, he had heard stories of the magical waters of Validaan. It was said that they prolonged life, healed injury and illness, and reflected the future, even the future that might have been. Swallowing hard and taking a deep breath Lukas continued along the path moving deeper into the garden.

III

After several minutes the path turned sharply to the right and headed due east. He continued walking for about fifteen minutes at a quick pace until he could see the eastern wall of the garden peeking through the shrubbery. Up ahead the path opened into a round courtyard. A bubbling stone fountain stood at its center with crystal-clear water pouring down its sides in even sheets. Before the stone wall on the easternmost edge of the courtyard was a massive tree. It flourished with bright yellow leaves and golden fruit hanging from thick branches. A parrot perched in one of the branches, and below the parrot stood a young man in the purple tunic of a serf. His long black hair tied in a ponytail hung halfway down his back.

Lukas approached slowly and heard the parrot speaking to the man: "Go ahead, lad," the bird screeched, "take an apple!"

The young man hesitated. Like Lukas, he had been given the Law upon entering the garden, so he peered around nervously to see if the serpent was watching. He then glanced over his shoulder and saw Lukas standing motionless beside the streaming fount. "No, thank you," the man answered loudly for Lukas's benefit. "I'm not . . . hungry."

The bird's bright orange head turned toward Lukas for a moment and then back to the young serf. "They're not to eat!" it squawked. "They're gold!"

Lukas squinted and stepped closer. Before he realized what was happening, he was standing beside the serf. The young man reached for the nearest solid-gold fruit. He plucked it effortlessly from the branch and almost dropped it because of its weight. His eyes shined as he held the smooth, golden apple close to his face and rotated it to catch the light of the garden.

Lukas gazed at him in wonder.

After a long silence the parrot spoke again. "There are seeds inside the apple. In a year they grow into another tree filled with golden apples." The bird squawked and flapped its bright green and yellow wings with excitement. "You will be rich forever . . . you and your children, and your grandchildren, and your grandchildren's children . . ." As the bird rocked back and forth on the branch, its words dissolved into an incoherent chirping and cawing.

The young man turned his fevered eyes onto Lukas and spoke to him in a low, trembling voice, "I've heard stories about an old man in Sardia who had such a tree."

Lukas said nothing. He had heard such stories as well, and now he was beginning to believe they might be true.

The bird stopped chirping and shouted, "Take it, lad! There's a secret door in the wall behind the tree. Nobody will see you leave." Its chirping at that moment sounded suspiciously like laughter. The young man, still staring at the golden apple, moved instantly toward the wall. A small door covered in vines swung open allowing the man to leave in silence.

The bird cocked its head, ruffled its feathers, and looked directly at Lukas with its piercing yellow eyes. "Plenty more, young man, plenty more!"

Lukas took another step toward the apple tree and reached out to touch it. At that moment a memory flashed through his mind. Just yesterday he had reached out to touch Princess Lilia's soft cheek when he asked for her hand in marriage. As his finger touched the golden apple, its surface was hard and cold. He knew it could never replace his love for the princess.

Lukas withdrew his hand and looked up at the bird. "No," he said, "a treasure far more precious than gold is waiting for me."

"What could be more precious than gold?" the parrot screeched. It stomped up and down the branch. The tree trembled and several golden apples dropped to the soft ground with a thud.

Lukas backed quickly away, bumping into the fountain. As he turned, a vision in the glassy stream of water caught his eye. He saw himself in a room filled with gold, precious gems, and priceless treasures. He sat alone, old and sad, reflecting on a life filled with everything gold could buy but with a heart that was completely empty. When he closed his eyes, the image vanished. Without even a glance toward the shrieking parrot he set out again upon the winding path.

IV

Nearly an hour passed and twilight descended on the Garden of Validaan. Lukas continued along the path as it was illuminated by the light of a rising moon. As his legs grew weary and his eyelids began to fall, he was suddenly roused by the sound of festive music ahead.

Squinting through the darkness he saw brilliant lights piercing the dense foliage. The garden opened onto a wide, green lawn with a large, white gazebo covered in vines and pink blossoms. Inside the gazebo brightly lit by glowing lanterns three handsome men danced with three lovely maidens to the music of a string quartet. On the far end of the patio three more young women sat expectantly in ornate white dresses. Beside them sat an older woman who immediately leapt to her feet and approached Lukas with a wide smile.

"Welcome!" She clasped Lukas's hand and led him up the three hollow steps onto the dance floor. "My daughter, Claire, is waiting for you!"

"Claire? Waiting for *me?*" Lukas uttered half to himself. When young Claire rose from her seat with a shy smile, Lukas's hunger fled from him. Before him stood the most beautiful young woman he had ever seen. His heart melted and his thoughts raced in a thousand directions as he momentarily lost his ability to breathe. Fire ignited inside him, and he suddenly longed to dance.

"Claire," the mother said, "we have a visitor. I believe he's about to ask you to dance." She looked at Lukas hopefully.

He started to agree, but a stray memory emerged from a cluttered corner of his mind, a promise he had made to Lilia at the Spring Festival the day before. After their engagement dance he had promised Lilia that he would never dance with another.

Lukas glanced down at the floor. "No," he said, "I cannot. I have promised my heart to another."

The old woman inched closer and touched Lukas's chin, lifting his gaze toward her daughter. "Then keep your heart," she urged in a plaintive tone, "but give your hand to my Claire for just one dance."

Lukas looked deeply into the maiden's eyes, and the strength of his promise began to wane.

When the matron spoke again her words were numbing, "Who knows? Perhaps your heart will change when you look upon the fair face of my daughter for a time." She took Claire's soft, white hand and placed it in Lukas's. Without hesitation Lukas reached out and grabbed Claire's other hand and gazed longingly into her deep, blue eyes with an enchanting smile.

"And very fair you are, young Claire," Lukas said, "but farewell nonetheless. Both my heart *and* my hands are promised to Lilia."

As the smile left Claire's face, the music stopped and the dancing ceased. All eyes were fixed upon Lukas as he turned and left the gazebo. For a moment Lukas hesitated, glancing back at Claire and her frowning mother, but then he hurried along the garden path as the music resumed.

A short time later Lukas stopped at the sight of a small waterfall spilling into a babbling brook. In the shimmering moonlight he saw what might have been — he and Claire twirling and spinning in a wedding dance while Princess Lilia sat hopeless and brokenhearted in the darkness of the dragon's cave. Shaking the vivid image from his head his hunger and thirst returned. Forcing one foot ahead of the other he continued his journey along the path.

V

Minutes later Lukas turned a corner, ducked under a large tree limb that hung low over the way, and stopped abruptly at the end of the garden path. On his right a door led out of the walled paradise and before him on an unguarded, marble pedestal sat the Helmet of Validaan. He began to reach for the prize, but then he hesitated. The words of his vow to the serpent played back through his mind: *You must swear an oath that you will not remove anything from the garden, neither plant nor herb, water nor rock.*

"Why not take the prize, lad?" a voice hissed from the shadows. Suddenly the snake reappeared slithering down the branch of a tree.

"I would," Lukas confessed, "if I hadn't promised you that I would not remove anything from the garden. As much as I need the Helmet, I am neither a thief nor a liar."

The snake hissed, "Countless travelers with as much temperance as you have made it this far into the garden only to snatch the Helmet and lose their lives!" After a deliberate pause the snake continued, "The temperance that controlled you has also set you free. You're free from the Law, my lord. Now go. You may take the Helmet of Validaan with you. It rightfully belongs to you."

Lukas's eyes widened, and he swiftly lifted the Helmet from the pedestal and lowered it onto his head. As he did so, he noticed a small, silver flask no larger than his hand resting on the marble column.

The snake spoke from behind: "Take the flask as well. It's always filled with the cold, enchanted water of Validaan. Its everlasting source of water will quench your thirst in even the driest regions of the world."

Lukas took a long drink from the flask before attaching it to a ring on his belt. The water instantly satisfied both his hunger and thirst, filling him with indescribable energy. The snake added, "There's one more item of importance. You will find the second portion of your map in a small box beneath the pedestal."

Lukas stooped to retrieve the second fragment. Aligning the new piece of the puzzle with the left edge of the first segment, the map continued as did the foreign message along the bottom:

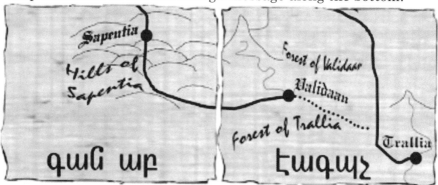

Turning to the snake which had slithered closer, he asked, "Can you read this language?"

"Dwarfish," he hissed, "of course. Their language reads from right to left. It says *kogah ba nag,* 'strength is in attaining.'"

Lukas played the strange message through his mind: *Does this mean that I need strength to obtain the weapons or that obtaining them will bring me strength? Maybe both are true.* He carefully placed the map fragments into his front vest pocket. Lukas thanked the snake for his help and bid him farewell before leaving the Garden of Validaan.

Reviewing the second portion of the map once again in the light of the moon, he traced the route west, and then north to his next destination, the Halls of Sapentia, where a sword of power could be found. The journey would require two full days of travel which he would begin at the first light of dawn.

He slept in peace outside the walls of Validaan. He had faced his first challenge and had succeeded. He dreamed of success—the sword, shield, and armor won by little effort, the dragon fleeing from his presence in fear, Lilia embracing him and praising his valor, the whole Kingdom of Trallia secure and prosperous under his wise and righteous reign. His dreams held no fire, heat, or smoke.

The following morning Lukas awoke awash with pride and confidence. He felt invincible.

Chapter Three

The Halls of Sapentia

I

While the sun and moon greeted each other at daybreak, Lukas refreshed himself from the flask of water he had received in the garden. With renewed energy he followed the remains of a road west out of the Valley of Validaan. At times he had trouble following the overgrown path as it wound through the bushes and trees, but within hours the trail gradually climbed out of the valley and opened onto a vast expanse of green hills. Though Lukas was unaware of it, he had already entered the realm of Sapentia and traveled well within its borders where tall oak, maple, and pecan trees dotted the grassy knolls.

Six hours later as the sun began to descend through the sky, the path he followed began to gradually curve to the north. He could spot what looked like a dark smudge on an otherwise perfect landscape of rolling hills. A few hours after that, his eyes began to make out the structural outline of a large series of buildings peeking through a dense grove of hardwood trees, though it was still many miles away.

As evening settled on the hill country, Lukas set up camp between two trees and slept peacefully. Early the next morning, he awakened to the smell of wild strawberries growing nearby and the sound of squirrels foraging for nuts in a walnut tree above him. After packing his things while the horizon was still a pearly gray, Lukas continued northward as the rising sun caused the dew on the grass to sparkle like diamonds.

He trudged up and down the hills for several hours until a lofty stone castle gradually rose into view. Though he felt no fear, his awareness had been sharpened by his travel through Validaan, and he fully expected to face some test of strength, courage, or wisdom. Unfolding the second map fragment once more he confirmed that the palace before him was, indeed, the Halls of Sapentia. If he moved quickly, he would arrive within the hour.

After taking a long draught from his silver flask Lukas picked up his pace and ascended the trail with renewed vigor. Though the noontime sun shone through the budding trees, the ground still felt cool to his feet and the smell of dew filled the air. The sun appeared to move lazily in this peaceful land, and Lukas hoped that he might hold the Sword of Sapentia before the sun began to set in the cloudless sky.

In less than an hour Lukas neared the unguarded castle grounds. He quietly crossed over an ancient stone bridge spanning a shallow creek that seemed to be whispering in conversation with the rustling leaves of the maples, oaks, and elms that adorned its banks. Through the trees Lukas spotted the main entrance, a simple oak door decorated with wood carvings that had lost their sharp edges centuries earlier.

Before he had decided whether or not he should knock, the door opened with a slow, creaking sound, and a tall, old man ducked through. He wore a long maroon cloak and hood that highlighted his white hair and beard. "Good morning, young one," he said in a kind but deep voice. "I'm Lord Custor, twelfth and final steward of Sapentia."

Lukas bowed his head slightly in respect. "I'm Lukas of Trallia, son of Stanton."

"Welcome to the Halls of Sapentia, Lord Lukas," Custor said with a smile. "You've arrived just in time. Four other men are waiting patiently inside to try their hand at the sword. That is your reason for coming here as well, correct?"

"Yes, my lord," Lukas answered with disappointment, afraid that another man more valiant that he would leave with the sword before he could.

Lord Custor placed a large, gentle hand on Lukas's shoulder and said, "Don't worry, lad. You shall receive your chance. Brave knights have been trying to win the Sword of Sapentia for centuries, and yet none have been able to acquire it."

These words, though meant in comfort, alarmed Lukas even more.

The steward grinned broadly, and as they passed through the doorway into the torch-lit foyer he advised, "It is not a difficult task in itself, young one, for the one who has wisdom. The Sword of Sapentia has rested in this castle for centuries awaiting the one destined to wield its power. Who knows? Perhaps Lukas of Trallia, son of Stanton, is the one for whom it was forged and hidden. Come now, your time is short."

Lukas followed the old man through a straight and narrow hallway lined with paintings of the former stewards and stewardesses of Sapentia. There were twelve in all — men and women whose faces bore a stern countenance but whose eyes looked down with kindness. The last painting, the twelfth, was that of Lord Custor himself.

At the end of the hallway Custor heaved open a solid oak door that groaned on its iron hinges as if opening it were a great bother. It revealed a vast stone hall aglow with sunlight pouring through vibrant, stained-glass windows. The images in the windows were identical to the paintings in the corridor, twelve men and women. Even Lord Custor's visage had been fashioned in stained-glass. Lukas was so enthralled with the artwork that he did not immediately realize that the walls of the great hall were covered with dozens of swords.

II

As Lord Custor had mentioned, four other men stood in the center of the great hall waiting for the steward to return. As Lukas entered, the others regarded him with either contempt or indifference and then continued to scan the swords that adorned the four walls.

"Thank you for waiting, gentlemen," said the steward. "This is Lukas of Trallia. He's seeking the Sword of Sapentia as well."

Lukas bowed slightly in respect before turning his own attention to the walls. The swords – all of them shiny and new – were of every color, size, shape, and style, each of them unique in beauty and craftsmanship. Lukas then noticed that six smaller doors covered with swords opened out of the main hall, presumably leading to the rest of the castle.

"Now," Custor said to the five men, "let's begin. You shall each have one opportunity to select the true Sword of Sapentia. As you can see, there are dozens to choose from, but only *one* is real."

The men continued to scan the swords wondering which one to choose.

"I give you all the same advice: use prudence and wisdom. If you choose the right sword, it will be yours. But if you choose the wrong sword, this ancient verse will be fulfilled:

Two sounds will echo from the floor

And you will be a man no more

For upon the wall a second sword

Will hang where there was only one before."

Silence settled on the hall as all five men gave their full attention to the steward. His words were solemn and his expression grave. He spoke, "Again I warn you: once you remove a sword from the wall, you must live with the consequences of your choice forever. If destiny is on your side, you shall leave with the Sword of Sapentia in your hand. But if this is your day of doom, you shall become a sword, left to hang on the wall for ages . . . as all of the swords you see before you . . . all, of course, but one. Yes, those past adventurers were brave," he said, pointing at the swords. "They were very brave, but very foolish!"

Suddenly one of the young men looked down at the marble floor, and trembling, strode briskly out of the room. As the oak door slammed shut with a deep thud, the Lord of Sapentia asked, "Are there any more who wish to leave and seek either doom or destiny elsewhere?"

The other men stood firm. For a moment Lukas thought he

might lose courage, but he drew a measure of confidence from his success in Validaan, and he set his mind upon the challenge.

The steward hesitated just a moment longer and then answered with resolve, "The first to arrive will make the first choice: Prince Julius of Magnus, choose your sword."

Prince Julius wore a long, blue cloak that shimmered as he walked. His blonde hair flowed back from his brow in feathered waves and was held firmly in place by a blue beret. With bright blue, hawkish eyes he examined the four walls of swords for several minutes and finally set his gaze upon one sword in particular. As blue as the mantle he wore, the sword shone bright as a summer sky.

"That's it. The blue sword," he said. "I know it is the one."

Prince Julius slowly reached forward and grabbed the sword in his blue-gloved hand. Pulling it from the wall he examined it in the dim, orange light that sparkled through a stained-glass window above him.

Cling!

Clang!

Two blue swords fell to the marble floor. Lord Custor quickly hung both swords on the wall. Then he turned to the second knight and smiled.

"Lord Daniel of Sardia, you'll choose next."

III

With wide eyes and a pale face Lord Daniel stepped forward. Tall and strong, he wore heavy, silver armor that shined brilliantly in the colorful light of the hall. His dark hair flowed over the fine, red cape on his shoulders. Lord Daniel wandered the hall of swords for several minutes, his silver armor clanging with each step. He finally stopped before the largest sword in the room — a sword as tall as he — with a handle large enough for four hands.

He declared proudly, "If this is not the famous blade, then the Sword of Sapentia is not worthy of me!" Without hesitation Daniel grabbed the sword with both hands and pulled it from the wall.

Clung!

Clunk!

Two massive swords fell to the floor. The old steward retrieved them and attached them to the wall as if they were as light as reeds.

Lord Custor turned to the third man. "Prince Formosa of Delphilo, it's your turn to choose."

The third man wore light, delicate clothing of radiant colors with fancy cuffs and a frilly collar. His thin lips, normally curled into a pleasant smile, now bore an anxious frown. Walking briskly back and forth over and over again he nervously examined the swords. Just as Lukas and the steward began to grow impatient, Prince Formosa stopped before one particular sword, placed his hands on his hips, and stared at it for a long time, uneasily biting his bottom lip. It was long and bright with ornate decorations carved in the blade and jewels encrusted in the hilt.

"This sword," Formosa said, "is the most beautiful work of art I have ever witnessed. I cannot imagine the Sword of Sapentia could be more beautiful than this one." When he clasped the handle with his soft hands, a smile of pleasure returned to his face. He closed his eyes and pulled the sword from the wall.

Ching!

Chang!

Two delicate sabers fell to the floor. Lord Custor gently placed them both on the wall and turned to Lukas who stood alone in the center of the room.

"Lukas, you may choose."

Lukas hesitated, closing his eyes and clearing his mind of the looming dread. Instead of beginning with an examination of the swords, he turned to the steward and asked, "Are these all of the swords, my lord, or are there others to choose from?"

The steward smiled. "The six doors lead to six more rooms of similar size. Each room is filled with swords."

"Then," Lukas said, "I'd like to examine *all* the swords before I choose."

Lukas spent the next half-hour moving from room to room.

Each hall was filled with blades of so many different sizes and shapes that it made him dizzy and uneasy. *Which should I choose?* he anxiously thought.

At the farthest end of the hall Lukas discovered a small seventh door. He opened it carefully. The soft, pine door creaked loudly, and the musty draft caused long-dormant cobwebs to dance gracefully in the corners. Lord Custor followed closely as Lukas entered the final chamber.

"In the beginning you said all of these swords except one were once men who had chosen foolishly?" Lukas questioned the old man who nodded in response.

"That should mean the true Sword of Sapentia would be the oldest," Lukas mused.

He began a close examination of the swords hanging on the walls. They were covered with dust and cobwebs. Lukas neared one particularly old, rusty sword hanging in the center of the wall. It was devoid of decoration, long and skinny like an elderly beggar, and it looked as if it would disintegrate with a touch.

"This is certainly the dustiest and rustiest sword of them all," Lukas said. "It has been hanging in this castle longer than any of the others." He stepped forward, put his hand on the hilt, closed his eyes, and pulled the sword from the wall.

IV

Immediately the decrepit sword began to glow. The rust evaporated and the sword suddenly changed into a beautiful blade of radiant silver.

The old steward beamed. Handing Lukas a jeweled sheath Custor said, "The Sword of Sapentia is now yours, Lukas. Wield it with the wisdom and prudence by which it was earned."

Lukas gazed with wonder at the sword and then stared at its place on the wall. Behind the sword a small square of parchment had been hanging for centuries. Snatching it from the wall Lukas lined up the third piece of the map with the top edge of the second. His world had grown considerably larger: the map led him to continue heading due north from Sapentia into the Trembling Mountains. Lukas also noticed the continuation of the message in the ancient script:

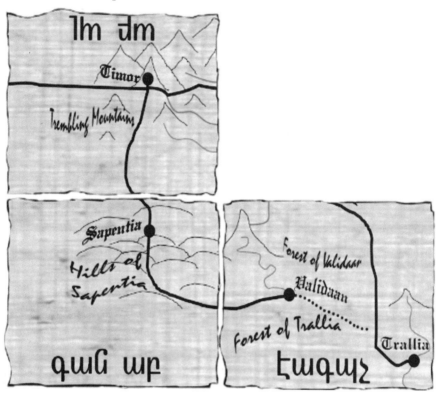

"Lord Custor, can you read Dwarfish?"

Custor peered at the text and nodded. "Yes, my lord. The left-handed dwarves write their language from right to left. It says, *kogah ba nag, lo ba.* It's missing a final word, but the message so far translates, 'Strength is in attaining, not in. . . .' The fourth piece of the map should complete the sentence."

Lukas asked, "Do you know what that means . . . 'obtaining power is strength'?"

"No. But you are misinterpreting the message. It *does not* say, 'Strength is in *obtaining*,' but 'strength is in *attaining*.' There is a vast difference."

Puzzled, Lukas said quizzically, "I do not understand. What is the difference?"

"*Obtaining* refers to winning a prize, gaining something. But *attaining* refers to reaching a goal, accomplishing a feat."

Looking down at the strange scribbling Lukas pondered Custor's words for a moment. Placing the map segments in his pocket, he glanced again at the empty space on the wall. One unanswered question still lingered.

"Is something troubling you, my lord?" Custor inquired.

"Yes. If the Sword of Sapentia was once alone on the wall, why didn't the first seeker acquire it since there was no false blade to choose?"

"The blade was not false," Custor said. "It was the man. Note this well: if the impure and foolish take hold of the Sword of Sapentia to claim it as their own, they will be turned into blades of falsehood. The truth is . . . until this day no man or woman would have been able to wield this blade. It has waited for you and you alone. It is your destiny. Now the Halls of Sapentia will be emptied, and the great line of stewards will come to an end." With a bow, Custor bid Lukas farewell. "Providence and blessings will be upon your journey, my lord, as they have been even until now."

Moments later Lukas triumphantly emerged from the dim foyer of the castle holding the sword before him to catch the bright rays of the late afternoon sun. As he stepped across the threshold of the doorway into the open air, the ground began to shudder. The castle shook and hundreds of swords fell from the walls, crashing on the stone floors like thunder echoing through a deep valley.

One by one the false swords were changed into brave but foolish men and women. Rubbing and shielding their eyes, they emerged from the dark castle into the bright daylight. The bewildered crowd filed off the castle grounds toward the main road, wondering how long they had been slumbering and still hoping to find the magical sword they had originally sought.

Lukas once again consulted the map and plotted his course north to the ominous Trembling Mountains. He had far more than when he had departed Trallia. On his left hip hung the Sword of Sapentia, on his right the silver flask from the garden, and his head was covered by the Helmet of Validaan. Beyond these material things his experience in Validaan had given him confidence in his abilities, and his time in Sapentia had bestowed upon him the assurance that destiny was, indeed, on his side.

That night after making stout progress hiking northward over the hills of Sapentia, Lukas slept – and dreamed.

In his dream he stood on a vast, grassy plain armed with the legendary sword, shield, helmet, and breastplate. The three knights from the Halls of Sapentia encircled him and challenged him to hand-to-hand combat. With swift strokes each of the three men was disarmed. Their swords dropped to the ground with a loud noise. A moment later they all turned and fled.

As he looked up at the horizon, Lukas saw Lilia approaching still dressed in her delicate garment from the Spring Festival, the red amulet of betrothal dangling around her neck. She was smiling as she came, her hair blown back by the light breeze that swept across the plain.

A moment later the breeze began to grow and Lukas soon felt a powerful, hot wind blowing on his back. When he turned to look behind, dread filled his eyes. He dropped the sword and shield and spun away to run from the wall of fire that raced toward him across the field.

When Lukas awoke the next morning, his heart pounding, he thankfully shook away the nightmare. It was just another dream.

Chapter Four

The Tunnels of Timor

I

The next day the optimism Lukas felt from his victory in winning the helmet and sword began to wane. He was troubled most of all by being alone. He had no traveling companion, no occasional stops at roadside inns, no place to hear or share a story. All the captives of Sapentia who had been released simply disappeared, each heading his or her separate way oblivious to the existence of the others. Lonely and perhaps even a bit lost Lukas trudged northward. Though he was not certain where he was, he knew he was not where he needed to be.

On the second day Lukas's surroundings finally began to change, and he realized that he had found the road again. He spent nearly seven hours climbing steadily. First he ascended a steep ravine out of the hill country of Sapentia; then the path became less steep but more rugged, pulling the strength from his muscles. The rocky incline was interrupted by deep trenches through which lava and water once flowed though now they were dry and dusty. Traveling north toward a jagged line of mountains he constantly examined the map. *I should be there by now,* he told himself, and yet each day the mountains remained distant as if the painted horizon were being pulled farther and farther from his reach.

At dawn's first light on the third day following his departure from the Halls of Sapentia, Lukas awoke, took a drink from his silver flask, and washed his hands and face. Then in astonishment he looked up to see that the gnarled, leafless tree he had camped underneath was actually a crooked signpost. Written in large, faded letters were the following words:

TRAVELERS BEWARE
You Are Entering the Land of the
Trembling Mountains

As soon as he passed the marker, the earth shook mightily beneath him. The tremors instantly reminded Lukas of the day the dragon attacked. He was terrified when he realized that this rumbling came from deep within the earth and seemed to be set off by his very presence. *No wonder nobody travels this road,* he thought, and a deep, angry quake followed as if in response.

Few plants and trees grew along this part of the road. No birds flew. No animals moved. Only large, biting flies buzzed around him trying in vain to find a way to bite through Lukas's helmet and green tunic. Soon the dusty road began a steep climb toward the nearest peak which was looming ahead at last. The Trembling Mountains looked like an army of giants guarding the passage to the north. Lukas could not imagine a way for a mortal to climb their sheer walls.

At midday when the sun blazed and the ground continued its brutal shaking, Lukas encountered the door. The black steel entrance to the Tunnels of Timor stood menacingly at the end of the road, built directly into the side of the mountain. To its right a smaller door stood open, and a tiny man emerged from the darkness.

"Welcome, traveler," he growled around his pipe, smoke curling gently upward from the glowing bowl. The dwarf's stern, bearded face surrendered a slight smirk as he unenthusiastically announced: "I'm Kraag, keeper of the keys, third trustee of Mount Timor, protector of the Armor, and so forth and so on. You either think you're braver than you really are, boy, or you're hopelessly lost." Taking a few small steps forward, he continued, "I hope, for your sake, that you're lost."

II

Kraag stood at only half of Lukas's height and wore heavy, dark clothes and a short, black cape. His head was uncovered, and his hair was thick like steel wire. When Kraag moved close enough, Lukas squatted down so he and the dwarf could look each other in the eyes.

"I'm neither lost nor particularly brave," Lukas answered. "I'm seeking the Armor of Fortis."

"Hah!" The dwarf laughed, turning toward his small door. "You'll find the Armor through that big door there," he said, pointing with his pipe, "at the end of a maze of tunnels too terrible for even the bravest warriors. Goodbye."

As Kraag disappeared through his small door, Lukas called out, "Wait! Aren't you going to let me in?"

The little man sighed and turned. "You truly want to enter the Tunnels of Timor?"

"Well, I do not *want* to. I *have* to."

The dwarf gave Lukas a doubtful look. "You have a choice now, boy. Take my advice . . . turn back now."

"Why?" Lukas whispered. "What's in there?"

Kraag's eyes widened. "Fear . . . terror . . . dread! None of my own people will go beyond the metal door. Nor will I. My grandfather chose to enter the tunnels. The next day my father became the trustee of Timor!" The dwarf's stony expression suddenly cracked into a myriad of wrinkles, and with deep laughter he said, "Why don't you just turn around and go back home, boy? No one has sought the Armor of Fortis and survived. All of those before you fled up the silver ladders like frightened children."

"The silver ladders?"

"The steel door locks from the inside. Once you enter the tunnels your only chance for escape is one of the three silver ladders that ascend to the top of the mountain. All are doomed to lose heart and escape through the mountain top . . . like that poor soul."

The dwarf suddenly pointed up the mountain slope. Following his finger Lukas saw two dwarves carrying a man down the side of the mountain. The man babbled nonsense and looked as though he had just endured the pain of torture.

"Go home now, lad," Kraag said, "and save my dwarves from carrying you down the mountain too."

Lukas glanced again at the two workers trying to maneuver the incoherent man. Would that be his fate? Or, as happened in the case with the sword, was he destined to conquer whatever awaited him in the Tunnels of Timor? Biting his lip, he smiled at Kraag. "Thank you for the warning, my friend, but I would choose to risk doom for what I seek. Please open the door."

The dwarf eyed him suspiciously. "Mark my words, boy. You won't obtain the Armor of Fortis, for no one has ever survived the tunnels. No one!"

Lukas began to lose patience with the gloomy man. "Very well then. I'll perish in the depths of the mountain, and your dwarves will have the evening off."

Kraag frowned. "There's no need for sarcasm, boy. My men will be waiting for you at the top of the ladders." He quickly unlocked the main entrance with a large key and opened the rusty door noisily. "You may take a torch from the wall."

Though he feared the flame, he would need light to find his way. Reluctantly Lukas snatched the smallest of three torches that hung at the entrance and held it as far away from himself as he could.

"Goodbye," Kraag said as Lukas stepped into the inky darkness. A moment later the door was rudely slammed shut with a crash and locked with a click of finality. Peering through the light of his torch, Lukas discovered a rusty, red, spiral staircase leading as far down as his faint light could penetrate. Grasping the railing in his right hand, he carefully began his descent.

III

The spiral steps were not nearly as long as he had first thought, and a few minutes later he stepped onto moist ground that squished under his feet. On his left stood a rusty door and on his right just a few feet from the corroded iron staircase, the rails and rungs of a silver ladder glimmered in the torchlight. "This must be the silver ladder the dwarf spoke of," Lukas whispered though his hushed voice echoed loudly in the stillness of the tunnel.

The silver ladder ended at a round, metal hatch in the ceiling. Curious, Lukas pushed his torch into the damp ground and climbed a few feet up the ladder to test the portal. It opened downward on a cleverly-crafted hinge without a squeak, and Lukas noticed that it did not have a latch to open it from the outside. Like the main entrance into the mountain, the hatches only locked one way. As he looked through the hatch, he saw another silver ladder climbing to a tiny circle of daylight far, far above — the top of the mountain. Releasing his grip on the hatch, a spring hinge instantly slammed it shut with a loud crash. Lukas jumped from the ladder, snatched his torch from the floor, and approached the rusty, metal door.

Grabbing the handle he pulled with all his might, and the door groaned as it opened. Lukas was instantly plunged into total darkness when his torch was extinguished by a draft of air that flowed through the doorway. For a few minutes he attempted to blow the fading embers of his torch back to life, but each breath seemed to merely pass into darkness.

Feeling his way through the dark, he was able to prop open the door by wedging the cooling torch into the base of its hinge. As his eyes adjusted in the new darkness, he realized that he actually could see, for the silver ladder behind him glowed with a faint white light.

With his left hand resting firmly on the hilt of his sword and his right reaching out in front of him, he forsook the temptation to climb the ladder and stepped warily through the doorway. Lukas did not fear the dark itself though he could not help imagining the nasty and dangerous things that might be lurking in it.

Then the noises began. To his left he heard something move against the stone wall while on his right heavy footsteps thumped on the muddy ground. "Who is it?" he said, whirling around and reaching for his sword. No response came, but the footsteps ceased. "Is anyone there?" Lukas asked again, louder this time.

Suddenly the wings of a bat or bird or some other hideous creature flapped in front of his face and over his silver helmet. Lukas drew his sword and slashed violently through the room striking nothing but air. He then swung the sword in a full circle. It did not touch anything. Unsure if he was in a wide tunnel or a vast cavern, he cautiously took another step forward. As he continued, the ground became softer and more and more damp, until he could feel cold water seeping through his leather shoes. If he stood too long in one place, he began to sink into the mossy ground. As he waved his sword before him, carefully navigating the wet soil, he wondered how so much dirt came to be in this cavern. A second later he no longer cared.

Lukas suddenly dropped into a pool of mud. He was up to his neck in the morass before he could turn around and begin to climb back onto firmer ground. As he grasped the wobbly edge of the dark pond, he felt a creature slithering around his feet and then another nibbling at his legs. Panicking, he tossed the sword a few feet ahead of him and pulled himself from the pool as quickly as he could.

As he crawled forward like a blind man feeling the ground with his fingertips as he searched for his sword, he heard more thumping footsteps, a buzzing noise behind him, then what sounded like a low growl somewhere on his left. He lifted his eyes and saw the faint glow of the silver ladder through the doorway — a remote beacon of light in a sea of darkness. As if floating in nothingness, the rails and rungs of the ladder emitted an inviting glow summoning him to return and climb to the light of safety. For a moment Lukas thought he might answer the summons, but in that moment his hand fell on the hilt of the Sword of Sapentia, and his will was restored.

"I will survive this," he told himself through clenched teeth. At the sound of his voice, heavy footsteps began to move closer and the growl turned into a vicious snarl. A large animal with great snapping jaws leapt at him in the darkness, but with a swing of the sword Lukas struck a mortal blow. The creature dropped to the soft floor with a thump, like marble landing on a soft bed of dirt, while Lukas rose to his feet and started moving again. This time, though, he used the sword to test the ground before each step.

Creatures continued to stir in the darkness. He heard something slither behind him, several small animals scampered away as he approached, and more deep growls rumbled in the distance. Thick spider webs clung to his helmet and clothing, but Lukas pressed on not sure when, where, or even if he would finally emerge.

Just as he started making good progress, the ground beneath him began to shake as an earthquake rumbled through the mountain. Lukas lost his balance and collapsed while several rocks thudded from the ceiling. As the tremors continued, he tried to regain his balance moving forward, sideways, or anywhere except backward.

His knees weakened with each uncertain step into the blackness, and his back ached from stooping to test the ground. Suddenly the silver helmet on his head clanged against a rock wall. Using his hands to feel along the stone surface, Lukas found the entrance to a tunnel. Unsure whether or not he was supposed to go that way, he took a deep breath and turned into the passage.

Instantly his eyes rejoiced to see a faint light in the distance. The tunnel narrowed, the ground hardened, and Lukas's confident pace quickened. He had nearly made it through the darkness, and though he was wet, covered in mud, and shaking with dread, he was alive. As he neared the light, he recognized that two torches lit up a small room at the end of the hall similar to the foyer at the beginning of the dark cavern. Another metal door blocked the path, and beside the door stood the rungs of another silver ladder — his second chance to escape the Tunnels of Timor.

IV

Ignoring the ladder, Lukas uncapped his silver flask, rinsed dirt from his sword, and washed himself off the best he could in the dimly lit room. After swallowing a deep draught of fresh water he gathered his courage and opened the second door.

Lukas gasped at the sight before him. He stood on a rocky ledge no larger than a small fishing boat. A long rope bridge spanned a massive underground canyon. The deep crevice obviously rose to the top of the mountain for bright light poured down from above. Lukas could see the opposite end of the rope bridge tied to posts on a ledge that mirrored his own.

What troubled Lukas about this particular cliff, however, were the violent gusts of wind that blew through the canyon, howling like wolves at a full moon. The winds were so savage that the rope bridge twisted and creaked, tangling near its slack center before unwinding again. Swaying constantly to and fro, occasional ripples surged from its center until it snapped back again like a whip.

No one could cross that bridge, he thought.

As Lukas pondered the awful sight, the door behind him blew shut. Unlike the first door this one had a handle and could be opened again. This comforted Lukas deep inside for he knew he could still escape up the silver ladder if he could not go on.

After checking to be sure his belongings were firmly secured, Lukas swallowed, took a deep breath, and grabbed the rope bridge with both hands. The violent winds sprayed sand into his eyes, but he managed to inch forward, grasping the thick rope with white knuckles. The bridge stabilized for a moment as the winds subsided granting Lukas a chance to take several steps before the currents increased again.

The bridge rippled and bucked like a wild bull. A second later Lukas's right leg became tangled in some of the cross ropes and his left arm was caught in the main cable. The gusts intensified, and he was trapped in the bridge like a fly caught in a spider's web. As he desperately tried to free himself, the bridge suddenly buckled and he found both hands free. He flailed about grasping for the main rope. Regaining his balance, Lukas rushed back to the ledge just a few feet away and sat down to catch his breath.

This is impossible, he thought. *That's not a bridge . . . it's a noose!*

Lukas waited until the winds died down again before rising

to his feet. He had to try again. There was no other way. He could not give up his quest. *Perhaps,* he thought, *if I wait long enough the winds will settle down, and I can cross safely.*

Then, as if divining Lukas's thoughts, the mountain shook with a vengeance. Rocks dropped from above, sand and dust blew through the canyon, and a boulder tumbled onto the ledge while Lukas tried desperately to keep his balance. The raging winds returned, and this time they snatched the Helmet of Validaan from Lukas's head and hurled it into the air.

Lukas tried to catch it as the winds carried it over the edge of the cliff, but it was no use. He watched helplessly as his helmet dropped into the crevice. But his shock turned to surprise as a strong gust of wind blew the helmet into the air and out of the abyss, floating inches past his reach. It twisted and turned in the swirling currents of air and soared high above the rope bridge and over the yawning chasm, only to land gently on the ledge at the opposite side of the canyon.

Now what? he thought. The helmet resting safely on the other side seemed to stare at him. He had come to this place for the third weapon, the Armor of Fortis, but now he was down to just one. *I need to get that helmet back. I can't give up now!*

As he paced back and forth trying to decide what to do next, his shin struck the large boulder that had fallen onto the far side of his ledge. The rock was as high as his knees and weighed at least as much as he did. Stooping down and clutching the boulder, he heaved it off of the edge of the cliff with all his might, and it fell into the canyon.

Lukas looked on with amazement as the violent wind currents took hold of the heavy rock and sent it soaring into the air. Zigzagging across the vast expanse for a few seconds, the boulder suddenly landed beside the helmet on the opposite ledge with a dull thud.

With raised brows and a pounding heart, the thought of jumping over the edge entered his mind. *No,* he reasoned, *it's too risky. What if I fall?* He looked down into the crevice which appeared to have no end. *I can't do it.*

Lukas re-opened the door behind him and saw the silver ladder. He had no choice. Perhaps he could find another way across the chasm. Perhaps another passage in the dark cavern would lead him to a better path. Or maybe he could reason with the dwarves and prove his worth in another way. Then from out of nowhere, Lukas recalled the words that King Lundin spoke when Lilia had been snatched by the dragon: *She needed you, lad. . . . She needed your valor. . . But you fled.*

Without a second thought Lukas spun around and jumped over the edge of the cliff.

At first he dropped like a stone sinking to the bottom of a lake, but the sensation of falling turned to flying as a sudden violent gust caught him and lifted him up past the ledge, beyond the rope bridge, and far up into the heights of the ravine. He tumbled through the breadth of the deep until a horizontal wind seized his form sending him soaring toward the landing at the opposite end. The bolder and helmet appeared to rush toward him, the rope bridge flapped below, and a second later he landed on the ledge and rolled hard against the door.

Bruised, scratched, and trembling with excitement, Lukas pulled himself to his feet. More than ever before his feelings of confidence grew into a sense of destiny, and somehow he knew this mountain would not defeat him. Smiling with both relief and pride he replaced the Helmet of Validaan on his head and passed through the next door.

V

Lukas clung to the contours of a narrow tunnel as he wound down a steep decline and turned a sharp corner. Up ahead a faint, red glow warmed the passageway. Hoping to find an exit, Lukas quickened his pace as the glowing intensified. A few seconds later the tunnel opened into a tiny anteroom with another metal door. This one had a small, square window through which a bright, orange light beckoned. To his right the rungs of the third silver ladder led to an escape hatch. He ignored the ladder and approached the window instead.

Just inside the door a massive cavern burned with fire. Streams of lava ran through the cave like immense veins, pools of molten rock boiled, tossing thick red magma to the ceiling, and fountains of flames burst from the floor and walls while black smoke billowed into the air. Though a path wound through the midst of the cave to a doorway on the other end, the flame, ash, and steam prevented any real hope of crossing.

Lukas began to tremble. His hand reached for the door handle but shook too violently to grasp it. His knees weakened, and his legs buckled. A moment later he sat down on the floor covering his head with his arms and praying the fire and smoke would just disappear. Buried memories flashed through his mind — bright flames and loud explosions, the terrified face of his mother reaching out for him, his father calling for help. But there was no escape.

After a few minutes trying to calm himself Lukas grabbed the door handle while he was still curled up on the ground. He opened it just a few inches and peered inside. The flames grew larger and the lava swelled. The heat singed his eyebrows in a single moment. His heart pounded harder and faster as explosions burst from the ground. Closing his eyes, Lukas pushed the metal door shut with a clank and calmly rose to his feet, sweat dripping from beneath his helmet, tears welling up in his eyes.

As if in slow motion, Lukas placed his hands on the silver ladder one after the other and climbed all the way to the hatchway. The door moaned as it opened, and Lukas ascended into the dark channel leading to the top of the mountain. Below him the hatch sprang shut with a clank that made him jolt. When the door closed, so did his window of opportunity to retrieve the Armor of Fortis and save Lilia.

A few minutes later Lukas emerged on the top of the mountain, gasping for breath.

"I knew you'd fail, boy," came the deep voice of the dwarf. He was sitting on a rock just a few feet away. "It's always the same. Nobody can make it through the Tunnels of Timor, though you made it farther than most."

Lukas threw himself on the cold rocky ground and began to weep.

Chapter Five

The Journey Home

I

"Where do you think you're going?" Kraag inquired casually when Lukas pushed his bruised and weary body up from the gravel. He had slept several hours into the night, and as the stars and moon shined brightly in the midnight sky, he stirred like a bear rousing from its winter sleep.

"I'm going home," he moaned.

"And what're you going to do about that dragon?" asked the dwarf. He puffed on his pipe, and the end glowed red in the darkness.

"The dragon . . ." Lukas whispered. "How do you know about the dragon?"

"It haunts you in your sleep. The dragon and the fire . . . Lilia and Taro . . . whoever they are all disrupt your sleep."

Lukas was on his feet, checking his belongings.

"It's all there, boy," Kraag groaned, jumping down from the rock. "Follow me. I'll show you how to get off this mountain." A deep thundering tremor suddenly sent small stones sliding down the nearby slopes before gradually subsiding. The dwarf ignored the rumblings and led Lukas along a rocky path as sweet smoke trailed from his pipe. Drawing in a deep breath, he spoke again: "The Sword of Sapentia and the Helmet of Validaan. Those must be worth something, hmm? I could get me a pretty price for 'em."

Lukas closed his eyes. He had come so far only to fail. With pain in each shuffling step he silently followed the little man along a narrow trail winding down the mountainside. Kraag had no need of a lamp to guide his way as dwarves could see as clearly in the dark as men see in the light.

When they reached the main road, the dwarf pointed toward the star-speckled horizon. "After about eight hours of travel in that direction you'll come to a winding road that runs north and south. If you turn south, it'll lead you along the Crevice of Kilgar bordering the eastern land of Lexor. You can follow that road all the way back home; it's about a week's journey on foot."

"And the way north?" Lukas asked.

Kraag frowned. "No, lad, that way's not for you. That's the dragon's land, and she treats trespassers far worse than you've been treated by Mount Timor." As if on cue, the earth shook again, a long but shallow quivering that caused the rocks and sand to rattle nervously in their places. The dwarf slowly turned and walked away humming an old, sad ballad as he faded into the darkness. Lukas watched him go until the dwarf's melody was smothered by the croaking of toads, and his pipe smoke was replaced by the dull scent of moss and mud.

Reluctantly Lukas set off toward a dark and unknown horizon.

II

Apparently Kraag's eight-hour estimate had been calculated in dwarf steps, for Lukas had reached the north-south road only six hours after departing Mount Timor. The earthquakes from the Trembling Mountains had passed with the night, but inside Lukas still trembled at the memories of darkness and flames. The new road ran along the western edge of the Great Crevice of Kilgar, a deep crack in the earth into which flowed all of the rivers from the western and northern mountains. At once he began following the road south toward Trallia. During the early morning hours the eastern rim of the crevice peeked through a yellow haze of fine sand that constantly blew from the east. In that brief period Lukas caught a glimpse across the canyon at the edge of the vast desert land of Lexor.

Lukas recalled the stories of Lexor he had heard as a child. Centuries earlier before the massive quake that opened the great crevice, rivers and streams had flown into Lexor feeding countless fresh water lakes. In those days it had been a bountiful paradise of fruits and grains with flourishing cities and villages, farms and fisheries. But when the earth cracked and the rivers dropped into the depths of the canyon, the land of Lexor dried into a harsh desert that rarely felt the cooling touch of rain.

Lukas understood the Desert of Lexor. A day earlier he thought his strength would never wane, that destiny was on his side. But last night a thought that had been rumbling in the depths of his mind for years erupted through the landscape of his life creating a massive fissure in his soul that left him dazed and confused. Though his feet carried him toward Trallia his heart wandered aimlessly unsure of where he should go or what he should do. Lukas had discovered a new meaning of the word "lost."

Lukas walked for several hours that morning pausing only to drink from his silver flask and adjust the sweaty clothes that stuck to his back and shoulders. Though he still drank from the enchanted water of Validaan, by breakfast time he was exhausted. He had slept but a few hours the previous evening on top of Mount Timor and had been walking ever since. Finding a lush patch of grass and trees growing on either side of a small brook, Lukas washed himself in the icy water and wearily followed it to the edge of the Crevice of Kilgar. There he saw the water plunge into the depths, some of it evaporating before it reached the bottom.

Returning to the roadside Lukas nestled himself into some tall reeds where he would be hidden from passersby on the road though he had not seen anybody at all since starting south that morning. Setting his sword and helmet beside him, he removed his outer cloak and covered the weapons. Then he rested his throbbing head in his hands and fell asleep. At first his sleep was deep as his weak body settled into the soft ground like a babe snuggling into his mother's arms. But soon the swirling impressions of bubbling streams and swaying reeds gave way to darker dreams.

Holding the Sword of Sapentia and wearing the Helmet of

Validaan Lukas stood in the center of a large hallway. Dancing flames and thick, black smoke closed in on him from every side. A few feet before him stood his father still dressed in his silk nightclothes. He turned to Lukas and shouted over the roaring flames, "Give me your sword, son!"

Lukas pulled the Sword of Sapentia from the sheath and slowly reached forward to hand it to his father who stood over him with terror in his eyes. The Sword of Sapentia shimmered and then began melting in Lukas's hand. Its silver metal dripped to the hardwood floor like wax retreating from an open flame. Lukas quickly pulled the helmet from his head and tried to give it to his father, but it, too, turned to liquid.

"But where are the armor and the shield?" his father shouted. He looked down at Lukas and his eyes turned from dread to disappointment. "I knew you would fail, son," his father said. "It's always the same."

"The . . . fire . . ." Lukas cried.

His father shook his head and frowned in disgust as the ceiling of the hallway suddenly exploded. A monstrous yellow claw shot from the inferno snatching Lukas's father and pulling him into the wall of fire. Instantly the floor below him gave way and Lukas began falling through flame, smoke, and heat. As he fell, total darkness engulfed him. He tumbled downward into a cool mist that covered his face like dew on a leaf and as he looked around he saw the sword, helmet, shield, and armor tumbling beside him. He desperately grabbed for them, but they were out of reach.

"Father!" he cried, his words echoing into infinity. "Father, they're all here! Come back!" He continued to fall, unable to snatch the precious weapons.

Lukas landed on the soft ground beside the brook with the thumping of his own heartbeat in his ears. He sat up. His racing heart slowed, but the thumping continued. Closing his eyes he heard what sounded like marching soldiers echoing through the canyon not far from where he lay. Upon further reflection he realized the marching actually came from the road just beyond the reeds. An army advanced north in the direction from which Lukas had just returned. Wiping his bleary eyes Lukas was shocked at what he saw.

Dressed in red and silver uniforms, the army of Trallia marched in perfect lines.

III

"Hello there!" Lukas hollered, stumbling to his feet and tripping onto the gravel road just feet from the rows of marching soldiers. Several footmen glanced at him, startled for a moment, but they believed him to be an unarmed vagrant and quickly decided to ignore him.

"I am Lukas, son of Stanton," he pressed, "Lukas of Trallia!" Desperate for somebody to acknowledge him he inched closer.

"You there," a voice called from the right, "step aside!"

Lukas turned to see a mounted knight commander slowly approaching from the head of the army. He wore the bright red cloak of the knights of Trallia, and a small golden helmet covered his head. The commander held the hilt of his sheathed sword with one hand, and Lukas knew his orders were meant to be taken seriously.

"My lord," Lukas said, approaching slowly with his hands held open before him. Being unarmed he knew the knight would not regard him as a threat. "I am Lukas of Stanton, ward of King Lundin."

The commander lowered his gaze and stared quizzically at the grubby, tattered figure. His horse whinnied and stamped at the gravel as the knight steered the black stallion around so he could have a closer look at the lad. After a moment, his face lit up with recognition. "Lord Lukas?"

Immediately the knight commander dismounted. Two of his fellow knights could now be seen lingering in the background, and they, too, dropped from their horses and approached. The knight signaled to his lieutenants, and they shouted an order for the army to halt. A moment later the marching ceased and the nearby brook could be heard once again.

The commander reached Lukas who stared back at him expectantly. "You *are* Lukas!" His voice could not conceal his astonishment. He bowed slightly in greeting. "I apologize. I am Lord Warrick of Karvil. These two men are my loyal thanes, Markus and Laedus." The two lieutenants bowed slowly. "My lord, we were told you had gone ahead to fight the dragon and had been killed!"

Lukas frowned. "I am obviously alive though I am weary and out of food." At that the commander gestured to his lieutenants who instantly began gathering a sack with provisions. "Who told you I had been killed?"

"Why, King Lundin, of course."

"I am alive." Lukas sounded like he was trying to convince himself. His gaze wandered for a moment before he met the commander's sky-blue eyes.

"Indeed! But you look ravaged as if you have been dragged behind a fleet of horses!"

Lukas blinked. He obviously looked the way he felt.

"Come," the commander said, "one of my lieutenants will give you a horse. You may ride at the head of the battalion with me."

Lukas scanned the battalion of Trallian soldiers, about five hundred men in all. "Where are you going?"

"We are joining the assembly of the army. The king ordered an attack on the dragon's lair."

"An attack on the dragon's lair?" Lukas responded.

"Surely the king told you he was sending the army!"

"No. I left very quickly. We barely spoke after the dragon attacked." In fact the king had specifically told Lukas that no army could destroy the dragon — *That was the purpose of my quest, wasn't it?* Lukas thought.

The commander explained: "The first line of archers and horsemen departed just hours after you left. They have all followed the same road. I am surprised you have not seen them."

Lukas mumbled, "I took another route." His mind was going in circles. Nothing seemed to make sense. "How many soldiers are assembling?" he asked.

"Most of the army . . . two thousand archers, the same number of footmen, and five hundred riders. We're going to slay the beast two days from now. The archers will shoot her from the sky, and the rest of us will finish her off." The commander's eyes lit up with excitement. "Just like the heroes of old . . . it will be spectacular!"

Lukas's eyes widened, and his face paled, "Oh no."

"What could be wrong? With so many warriors we're sure to defeat the dragon."

"No," Lukas declared, "you can not kill Haarlok with horses and arrows!"

"But of course we can!"

"No! Only the four weapons have the power to defeat her!"

"Four weapons? What are you talking about?"

"Did the king not tell you? Has he gone mad!?"

"What four weapons?" the commander pleaded.

"The Helmet of Validaan, Sword of Sapentia, Armor of Fortis, and Shield of Aequant. You need all four to defeat the beast. Any other attack will be in vain!"

The commander stared at Lukas, dumbfounded, shaking his head slowly. "Four magic weapons," he said thoughtfully. "My lord . . ." The knight beckoned his two aids with a slight gesture. "I am sorry to tell you this, but . . . the four magic weapons slaying the dragon . . . that is . . . well, that is an old myth. A story they used to tell children. Everybody knows it is only a legend."

IV

"No," Lukas insisted, "I know the weapons are real!" Lukas had hidden the sword and helmet in the reeds, but at the moment he thought it would be best not to tell the commander about them.

"Yes," the commander agreed, "they are real. But the weapons are relics from the past. They are only the sword and armor of Stefan, first king of Trallia. We all know he was powerful, good, and wise, but he distrusted his foolish heirs. He was convinced that none of his descendants would be able to rule in his place, his wealth would be squandered, and his kingdom would crumble as soon as he died. So upon his death his sword, shield, helmet, and armor were scattered throughout the world, and his descendants were challenged to retrieve them. For five hundred years none have been worthy of the challenge."

One of the lieutenants, Markus, broke in. "Of course, the Kingdom of Trallia never crumbled," he said proudly. "King Stefan's prophecy was wrong. His descendants prospered. They hunted down and slew the dragons. The nation is wealthy, and the army is powerful."

Lukas stood still as a statue. A knot formed in his stomach as he listened to their words.

The second lieutenant, Laedus, added, "Yet every ruler has pursued Stefan's relics in order to prove his worth. In the past Trallian kings have offered great rewards to anybody who could retrieve the treasures, but for the last hundred years their whereabouts have been nearly lost. All sorts of legends are told about them: they make you invincible, restore your youth, raise the dead, bring wisdom, slay dragons, work miracles. . . ."

Realizing that the story was troubling Lukas, Commander Warrick motioned for Markus and Laedus to be silent.

Lukas looked away surveying the footmen standing quietly at attention. His mind overflowed with questions. *Why did the king say I was dead? Why did he tell me the weapons could kill the dragon? Why did I believe it?* Now on the side of the road in front of all these soldiers the idea sounded ludicrous. Even King Lundin had admitted his story was "strange and fantastic."

Warrick concluded, "I am sorry, my lord, but no magic sword or enchanted shield will destroy Haarlok — only a hundred well-placed arrows in her belly. In the same way our forefathers destroyed the rest of the dragons. With two thousand archers I am confident we will celebrate a victory soon. Once again you are welcome to come with us."

Lukas closed his eyes. The words of King Lundin echoed through the corridors of his mind: *All four are essential in order to defeat this foe — she cannot stand against them.* Why would King Lundin lie to him? Did he want Lukas to retrieve the weapons for his own purposes? Was the king attempting to punish him for the loss of Lilia? Was he trying to be rid of him once and for all?

"Have I gone mad?" Lukas finally asked.

Nobody answered his question.

"My lord, Markus and Laedus have prepared two days' provisions for you. It is all we can spare. But they will be happy to provide you with a ride back to Trallia, if you wish. I am sure King Lundin would be delighted to see you alive."

"I am not so sure," Lukas mumbled. He grasped the sack of food and nodded his thanks.

"We can leave as soon as you are ready," Markus announced.

"No. That will not be necessary. I am walking from here. I am not sure I will be going home just yet. May fate be on your side when you face the dragon."

The commander shrugged and signaled for his officers to resume the march. "Well, my lord," he said, mounting his horse and nodding farewell, "wherever your adventures lead you may you have good luck."

Lukas continued to watch as the battalion marched out of sight. Then with a heavy sigh he returned to the reeds where he had placed his helmet and sword. He sat beside them for a long time just staring at the weapons. While he had spent his energy retrieving these relics of an ancient reign, an army of thousands gathered to make war with the dragon. While he had been sent into the wilderness on a vain quest, King Lundin sat in his palace awaiting the return of his Lilia. In the deepening silence on the road back to Trallia, Lukas held his head in his hands and wept bitterly.

All was now lost — even his hope.

V

Situated at its most narrow point was the only bridge that crossed the massive Crevice of Kilgar, and by midday Lukas passed its entrance on the western rim. A moment later something caught his eye just a few yards ahead. A thin, dark man with leathery skin dressed in tattered clothes lay on the side of the road trying feebly to drag himself southward. Lukas overtook him and attempted to walk far enough away so he could go unnoticed.

The old man sputtered, and his tired eyes rolled in their sockets. A moment later he set his cold gaze on Lukas. "Please," he choked, "help me!"

Lukas froze. Dust and sand covered the old man's ragged white beard and mustache and peppered his long, thinning hair. He looked so dirty and disgusting. Lukas wanted nothing more than to walk on by him.

"Who are you?" Lukas asked, without moving.

"I'm . . . I'm . . ." the man coughed and dropped flat on the ground under his own flimsy weight.

The man made no sound or movement. Was he dead? Lukas approached with a frown of annoyance on his face. As he drew nearer, he noticed the old man's rapid and strained breathing. With a strong hand Lukas turned the frail man onto his back and uncapped his silver flask.

Propping up his head enough to drink, Lukas placed the flask on the old man's lips. He coughed and gasped after each sip. Closing his eyes for a moment, the man carefully pulled himself from the ground with his elbows and looking at Lukas through bold, brown eyes, he said, "What kind of drink is that? Even my dimming eyesight has been restored!"

"It is the water of Validaan," Lukas said. He stood up and closed the flask. "It should get you far."

"Yes," the old man agreed, standing up straight, "it will lead both of us all the way across the Desert of Lexor." With those words he lifted his thin arm and pointed across the long, narrow bridge to the opposite end of the crevice.

"No," Lukas said, "I am on an important mission for Trallia. I cannot be delayed."

The old man grinned. "You are wrong. Four nights ago I saw you in my dream. You are the one who will return with me to Lexor and restore justice to our kingdom."

"No," Lukas repeated, "I am on a quest to save my. . . ."

"Your destiny is to free my people from the tyranny of King

Malif, to enforce the covenant, and to bring water for all."

Lukas clenched his teeth in frustration. "You must be confused," he said. "The heat has cooked more than just your skin. Farewell." Lukas turned and stomped away as the man just stared at him with a smile.

"Your sack . . . it has a loaf of bread, a bag of raisins and nuts, and three pieces of an ancient map."

Lukas stopped. Turning slowly toward the man, he said, "How could you know that?"

The man pointed at his head and his smile widened. "I saw it in my dream," he said. "I know you're haunted by your past, Lord of Stanton. But I have come to guide you to your future."

Chapter Six

The Court of Lexor

Even as he took his first step onto the long steel bridge to cross the Crevice of Kilgar, Lukas doubted the wisdom of following the old man. Just a few minutes earlier he was heading south on the road to Trallia. He had even sought to avoid the man lying on the side of the road, but ultimately the man's wild claim to have seen Lukas in his dreams lured him into this wild scheme.

"My name is Addis," the old man said, a new light of hope beginning to glow from his dark, weathered face.

Lukas stopped and glared at the man for a moment, and a thought suddenly struck him. "Wait a minute! How do I know you weren't hiding in the grass when the army passed? You could have heard me talking to the commander and seen the knights pack my bag."

Addis stopped limping across the bridge and pivoted on a bad left leg. He had convinced Lukas to follow him a moment earlier by revealing the contents of his sack, but they had only moved forward three steps before his young follower began to doubt. "You would like to believe that, wouldn't you?" Addis challenged

Lukas backed away. "Well, I am just not completely sure you dreamed about me or my bag. I have believed enough lies already on this journey, and I am tired of being played for a fool."

Addis squinted and took a step nearer. *"Being played for a fool?* What kind of fool passes the tests of Validaan? Or chooses the true Sword of Sapentia? How would I know those things? I *did* see you. I don't know how or why, but none of that matters. Truth is truth."

Lukas's eyes searched for something to look at rather than Addis's penetrating stare. A moment later a gust of sand from the eastern rim blew into his face. He blinked it away and with it all doubts about the old man's dream faded away. Looking up into Addis's eyes once again, he asked, "What else did you see in your dream?"

Addis smiled. "The future! Now come with me for I know where it lies. I'll tell you on the way."

"Where are we going?"

"To the Court of Lexor," Addis answered, "to see the so-called king." He turned and advanced along the steel bridge once again. "Come now, let's cross this bridge before even more doubts creep into your mind. Bridges are always the worst for doubts . . . neither here nor there . . . always in the middle. Hurry!"

The two men crossed over the bridge in silence. Though Lukas had a lot of questions, he was unsure about where to begin. About five minutes later after setting foot on the other side, Lukas stopped. His feet sank into the hot, white sand. "But this can't be right," he said. Addis noticed that Lukas sounded as if he were continuing a debate with himself that began somewhere at the midpoint of the bridge. He looked back at the lush, green region on the other side. "Are you sure this was part of your dream? It doesn't make any sense to go to Lexor . . . I have no business there . . . it doesn't fit."

Addis sighed, turning around again. "Where *should* you be going, then?"

"North, with the armies. Or . . . or south to the king. Or back to the Trembling Mountains in the west. But not this way."

"North, south, west," Addis said, shrugging. "You've no idea *where* you're going, do you? None of those ways seems better or worse than the others, right? So why not go east?"

"But this way is *wrong*. I can feel it."

Addis nodded. "Any other is a choice of the unknown too. It might be right; it might be wrong. But go east. That path is right no matter what the end."

"But . . ."

"Besides it's meant to be. Destiny has a grip on you now. You may choose a thousand paths, but you can only go one way. Now enough words. I have no more answers, so don't ask any more questions. We shall soon see how this journey unfolds. Lexor is two days away by foot. And please keep up. You have the water."

II

The two men sat on the edge of a rocky path taking turns drinking from the silver flask of Validaan.

If it had been possible for vegetation to grow in this region, the ancient road they were following would have been overgrown. But here several hours east of the bridge, there was nothing as far as they could see. Dry, crumbling soil covered the earth like a lizard's scales, and Lukas could picture an era long forgotten when this same desert had shimmered with miles of grasslands dappled with brilliant flowers. Yet that afternoon there was no sign of life, and even the drops of water that fell from the flask evaporated within seconds of touching the ground. The world of Lexor appeared lost and neglected beyond redemption.

As the two travelers rested in the midst of that dismal land, Addis continued telling the history of Lexor with a deep sadness in his voice. "Most of the people of this region left generations ago. Only one city exists today. It sits in the center of the wasteland ruled by King Malif. The road we're traveling is the only one that leads in and out of the city." He pointed at the red stone trail wide enough for a single horse and rider. "You see no source of water flows from here to the city, and no single person in Lexor could ever save enough of his own rationed water to cross the desert. King Malif enslaves the people of Lexor by giving each worker just enough water to survive. By the end of the work day we're thirsty and out of water again."

"Then how did *you* cross the desert?" Lukas asked as he capped the silver flask and reattached it to his belt.

Addis stood up, brushed dust from his tattered garments, and stared at the ground for a long time. Finally squinting against the light of the blazing sun, he said quietly, "Three men sacrificed their lives so I could make this journey to find you. Over the years the people of Lexor have learned to trust my dreams. Soon you will too."

When the two men resumed their trek along the rocky path, Lukas dragged his feet less than before. Doubts still lingered, but now they were mixed with determination. About an hour later when the flaming sun finally began to set, Lukas cleared his throat and asked, "Addis, what exactly did you see in your dream? What am I supposed to do?"

Addis stared into the deep, blue horizon where the first evening stars dotted the twilight sky. Limping along at a steady pace, he explained, "Before I get to that, you'll need to know a short history. Over a hundred years ago King Malif's grandfather . . . then the elected mayor of Lexor . . . made a covenant with the last one-hundred families left in the city. He dreamed up a plan to save the city by building towers that reached to the clouds to siphon water from the sky. Most of the families signed an agreement with the mayor to help build the towers. The others left and settled elsewhere. The covenant stated that as soon as the three towers were completed, the water would be evenly distributed, and each of the families would be owners of their own fertile land."

"Did the plan work?"

"Yes . . . perfectly. In fact once they began harvesting water from the sky the few rain clouds that used to shower the land from time to time vanished, lapped up by the towers. As a result, the people had more than enough water. But the mayor died before the covenant was enforced leaving his son to finish the work and return the land to the people. He broke the covenant and enslaved our families by rationing the water and keeping us all too frail to rebel. Forty years ago his son, Malif, became heir of the tiny kingdom. The original covenant had been carved into the foundation stone of the first tower for all to see. Today that stone makes up the eastern wall of Malif's throne room, and he's covered the writing with a wall hanging so no one might see. But we remember . . ."

After a minute of silence Lukas asked, "And how does your dream fit in?"

"You, my lord, will enforce the mayor's covenant." Addis furrowed his brow. Night was rapidly closing in and a strange chill began to descend across the desert. "I can't imagine how you'll dethrone King Malif," Addis confessed, "but in my dream I saw you giving water back to the people. The path you'll take to get there? That's still a mystery."

Lukas's heart stirred with compassion for Addis and his people. While following the grizzled old man as he limped along the barren road and listening to his story, Lukas nearly forgot the dragon, Haarlok, and his beautiful Lilia. Everything seemed so distant, so unreal. Of course that quest still lingered in the back of his mind, but at the same time his will and emotions were caught up by a different destiny — one that awaited him at the end of this rugged, desert road.

III

Lukas had never seen a more depressing sight. The city of Lexor consisted of the giant, walled palace of King Malif surrounded by tiny, cramped hovels – square, brick dwellings that housed the enslaved population. In the center and on the north and south edges of the city three massive stone towers stretched toward the sky, their sharp spires piercing the white clouds above. In the distance laborers worked to construct a fourth tower, and it was toward that new project that the workers marched as Addis led Lukas into the city around noon. Several peasants nodded to Addis as he returned, and a few stood and stared for a moment. Cautious whispers stirred all around, and within the hour the news that Addis had arrived with the man from his vision would reach even the workers at the top of the new tower. Hope had entered Lexor for the first time in a hundred years.

Less than a minute after arriving in the city, three menacing soldiers in black steel armor approached Lukas and Addis. Their armor was clanging and their black swords were drawn.

"Let me do the talking," Addis warned. "The older man in the center is the chief sergeant, Doro. He's a bit dim-witted, but he serves the king faithfully. Lexor only needs about fifty soldiers because they do their job well." Lukas nodded, allowing the old man to limp a few steps ahead as the three soldiers stopped several yards away. They eyed Lukas suspiciously.

Breaking an awkward silence as a gust of hot, dusty wind blew past, the sergeant shouted, "Halt!"

Having already stopped Lukas and Addis were unsure how to obey.

Addis swallowed hard and proclaimed: "Sergeant Doro, I have brought a visitor for King Malif. This is Lukas, son of Stanton, an ambassador from the Kingdom of Trallia."

The soldiers immediately began whispering questions to each other, and it was obvious after several seconds that none of them had any answers. It was also clear that Lexor had very few visitors, and the questions they were asking had never been asked before. "I am afraid that would be impossible," Doro finally responded. "And I am also afraid I will have to . . . er . . . take your weapon . . . I think." He pointed at Lukas's sword, raising his own black blade a few inches in an attempt to appear threatening.

Before Addis could respond, Lukas spoke loudly. "What kind of lord would surrender his weapon after such an unsure order?"

Chief Doro's eyes narrowed and his two soldiers looked up at him, lowering their own swords uneasily. As several passing citizens slowed their pace to eavesdrop on the confrontation, Lukas could actually hear the sound of armor rattling as one of the soldiers began to tremble nervously.

His confidence building, Lukas continued, "Now take me to King Malif, and I will forget your strange request."

The soldiers conferred again, and this time they nodded to each other in agreement. Addis shifted his weight back and forth from one foot to the other while Lukas slowly moved his right hand to the hilt of his sheathed sword. If it came to violence, he knew he would be able to disarm all three soldiers without shedding a drop of blood, but he was less certain that he would be able to protect

Addis in the fray.

"Um . . . you can follow us . . . my lord," Doro responded with a new humility in his tone. "All nobles are welcome in the court of the king . . . I think." Then his voice hardened again, and he pointed a black-gloved hand toward Addis. "But that *slave* must stay outside the palace walls!" The words sounded personal, and Lukas could tell that Doro and Addis had a long history.

Lukas eyed the old man who appeared to be relieved. As the three soldiers led the way toward the palace, Addis raised his hand in farewell, and Lukas winked in response. As soon as Lukas and the soldiers disappeared around the side of the castle wall, a small crowd of peasants immediately rushed upon Addis to hear the latest news.

Lukas's anxious escorts passed through several doors in the massive walls, and the dismal scene of Lexor was transformed before his eyes. The gritty sand and stone that characterized the city outside the palace was replaced by a lush, fruitful garden of trees and flowers. Decorative fountains adorned each corner, and the soldiers led Lukas over a stone bridge that spanned a pond filled with bright tropical fish.

The palace itself had been constructed of brown marble, but every inch was overgrown by bright green vines and yellow blossoms. "Watch your step," Doro grumbled as they ascended a short set of marble stairs over which a sheet of water cascaded, cooling their feet. At the head of the steps a massive wooden door opened into a long stone hallway. From one end of the hall to the other a narrow trench no more than a few inches wide had been carved to carry a shallow stream of water into the garden. Despite the perpetual drought experienced outside the palace walls water ran freely in the luxurious home of King Malif.

Two black-clad sentinels stared at Lukas and his escorts when they reached another massive door. A large hand gently touched Lukas's shoulder, and Doro said, "Wait here . . . er . . . Ambassador of Trallia." He approached the palace sentinels and, pointing at Lukas, explained the strange situation in hushed tones. One of the guards opened the door just a crack and slipped into the chamber behind it as the other examined Lukas curiously.

A few minutes later the door swung open without a sound revealing a bright, spacious room where King Malif sat isolated on a glistening, marble throne grinning at his unexpected guest. A large, handsome man in his fifties with dark hair and a well-trimmed beard, the king wore black garments, draping his shoulders with a stunning blue cape. Still too far away to speak to his guest, Malif smiled in silence as Lukas slowly scanned the luxurious chamber.

Green plants and colorful flowers grew in marble pots and planters arranged throughout the hall. Two small fountains on either side of the throne tossed sparkling flumes into the air that tinkled into shallow pools. The channel of water flowed from these pools through the throne room, down the hall, and out into the palace garden.

Just as Addis had described, the far wall of the room behind Malif's seat was actually the foundation of the colossal central tower that rose all the way to the clouds. Through a crystal window in the ceiling above the throne, Lukas could see the top of the spire puncturing the heavens, harvesting water that flowed constantly through the king's court. A solid blue tapestry draped across the far wall. If Addis's account was correct, the covenant was engraved beneath that covering. A single silver shield hung to the right of the tapestry as if to remind visitors that they were, after all, in the court of the king.

After ushering Lukas to stand several yards from the steps leading up to the throne, the three soldiers — including Doro — bowed low before the king and departed without a word. As the door closed, Lukas noticed that both sentinels had taken up positions in the throne room to keep an eye on their Trallian guest. Lukas bowed respectfully before Malif whose smile widened revealing a large gap in his crooked teeth.

"Welcome, Lukas of Trallia," he said in a deep voice. "I know why you have come." The king pointed to the silver shield hanging behind the throne. Looking back at Lukas with a sudden angry stare, he said, "You would kill me for it, wouldn't you?"

"*Kill you?*" sounded Lukas's first words to the king.

"Come now, Lukas," Malif groaned skeptically, rising from his seat. "You are the first Trallian envoy in fifty years. You have obviously come for the Shield of Aequant!"

IV

Lukas's eyes moved instantly from the king to the shield, one of the four weapons King Lundin told him he needed to defeat the dragon. He suddenly recalled his original quest to destroy Haarlok and save Lilia. Could it be that he had really found the Shield of Aequant just a few steps from his grasp? Could the old man's vision have led him here to fulfill the quest he had all but abandoned — the quest he had failed?

Taking two steps down from his raised throne, King Malif asked, "Why else would someone from the rich and powerful land of Trallia visit my dry and desolate realm except to rob me of my most prized trophy? Surely Lexor has nothing Trallia could ever want. We have nothing to trade . . . or plunder. And no one in their right mind would want to rule over this empire of dust where the only key to absolute power is a seasonal supply of water!" Malif laughed loudly for a moment before his face fell back into its habitual lines of discontent.

Though a confused series of questions spun around in his mind, Lukas showed no sign of worry or fear. Instead, almost without thinking, he reached down to his belt and unfastened the flask of Validaan. The sentinels, unsure of Lukas's intentions, slowly approached while King Malif eyed him cautiously, his own hand on the hilt of his long, black sword.

Lukas twisted the cap from the flask and drank deeply. He poured water on his hands, splashed more on his grimy face, then turned the flask upside down and let a stream of cool water drop from the spout onto the marble floor.

Puzzled, King Malif watched the water spill. A minute passed as he and Lukas stood locked in a long stare. The sentinels shuffled closer for a better look. Another minute passed and still the water flowed from the silver flask. A large pool formed quickly, winding its way to the channel that ran down the center of the throne room. After a third minute the tiny container of water showed no sign of emptying, and after the fourth minute one of the sentinels actually dropped his weapon, snapping King Malif out of his trance.

"W . . . where did you get that . . . that water?" Malif stammered staring wide-eyed at the unending stream that poured from Lukas's flask.

Lukas turned the flask upright and resealed the spout. "This flask is from the Garden of Validaan," Lukas answered, "and it remains forever full."

The king stood dumbfounded, caressing his black beard anxiously. Still gazing at the silver flask, Malif murmured half to himself, "What kind of devilry have those serpents of Validaan devised?"

With those words Lukas knew his silver flask and endless supply of water was a greater threat to King Malif's power than the entire army of Trallia.

"Give me the magic flask," the king finally said quietly, turning his eyes from the flask to Lukas. "Give it to me . . . as a gift."

"No," Lukas answered.

The sentinels inched closer. "We could take it from you, lad," the king said, his voice edged with anger.

"You could try," Lukas responded. He grabbed the hilt of his sword and glanced behind him as one of the guards slowly unsheathed his own weapon. "Tell your sentinels to back away. This is the Sword of Sapentia, and on my head is the Helmet of Validaan. Any man who challenges me in battle will quickly meet his doom."

Before Lukas finished his words the nearest guard drew his black blade and swung it hard at Lukas's back. "No!" the king barked, but it was too late. Almost without thinking, Lukas spun on his heel and sliced at the guard with his silver blade. To everyone's shock the guard instantly became lifeless sandstone.

"Fool!" the king shouted. He pointed at the second sentinel.

"Back away! That's the Sword of Sapentia! Who knows what other magical havoc it may wreak?" The remaining guard took several quick steps back and sheathed his sword.

"Your majesty," Lukas said, eyeing the new statue cautiously, trying to pretend he had fully expected its appearance. "I'm not here to kill you or to steal your decorations." He gestured toward the shield. "I want to reason with you . . . to bargain . . . providing, of course, a scoundrel like you is capable of a fair negotiation."

King Malif winced and backed away as Lukas took a few steps closer. "I am . . . I am a man of my word," the king lied.

"Not according to the report I have heard," Lukas retorted. "Nevertheless, I will give you the magic flask in exchange for the Shield of Aequant. . . ."

Malif nodded eagerly. "Take the shield! It's yours!" He stepped forward and reached for the flask.

Lukas pulled the flask away, and the king stopped in his tracks. "I'm not finished, your majesty," he said. He walked around the throne to the rear wall as Malif and the sentinel followed with their eyes. Lukas suddenly swung the Sword of Sapentia at the massive blue tapestry which instantly split in two and dropped to the floor. Just as Addis had described, the words of the covenant were revealed.

Horror filled Malif's heart, and he shook his head as Lukas spoke: "To complete the bargain, I also want you to honor the covenant of your grandfather. Free the people, and step down from the throne!"

The king's horror quickly turned to rage. "Get out!" he shouted, rushing behind the throne and snatching the Shield of Aequant from the wall. "I'll not trade my kingdom for a flask of water!"

Shaking his head in disappointment, a strong resolve welled up within him, and Lukas gripped his sword tightly. "Then you will become a stone memorial of your own wicked reign."

V

"GUARDS!" the king cried, backing away from Lukas.

Within seconds a dozen soldiers appeared from adjoining rooms wielding swords, spears, and bows. King Malif stepped back and watched, holding the Shield of Aequant firmly in his hands. A moment later Lukas was surrounded by soldiers on every side. They buzzed around him like swarming bees though several were turned to stone in seconds. Others dodged Lukas's blows and tried desperately to hit their agile target. One soldier managed to land his broadsword on the back of Lukas's head, but when it struck the Helmet of Validaan the black sword exploded into a million shards that blinded archers as they tried to take aim.

From one moment to the next total chaos became total silence. Both Lukas and Malif found themselves staring at a room filled with statues of warriors engaged in a fierce but futile battle. Lukas wound slowly through the statues and approached the king who had backed into a corner. "As you can see, the battle was over before it began."

The king scowled and lifted his own sword. "I do not believe so. Not even the Sword of Sapentia can harm a man who holds the Shield of Aequant. Its magic makes me invincible." The king stepped forward and slashed at Lukas. The blow was deflected, and he backed away. "See, boy?" he said, "We are at a stalemate. Neither one of us can win."

With a sudden stroke Lukas swung his blade at the king again. Sparks flew as sword met shield, but the king's defense was impenetrable. Lukas grasped his sword with both hands and swung with greater force to no avail. Again and again he slashed away, but everywhere he aimed the Shield of Aequant was there as if an unseen power moved it to protect its bearer. King Malif held his useless black sword in his left hand and the shield in his right, absorbing Lukas's tiring blows with ease. As Lukas's energy faded trying to pierce the shield, Malif began to cackle. "Give up, boy!"

Frustrated, Lukas held the Sword of Sapentia above his head and dropped it down on Malif with all his might. With a resounding clash, the force of the shield shot the sword from Lukas's grip, sending it spinning out of his hand, and into the air, landing at the feet of King Malif.

Lukas leapt to retrieve his weapon, but he tripped on a piece of tapestry that lay crumpled under his feet. Tumbling to the marble floor, he found himself on his back, staring at the sharp end of King Malif's black blade. Malif knocked the Helmet of Validaan from Lukas's head and rested the tip of his blade just inches from his throat. Panting heavily and sweating from exhaustion and fear, Lukas's eyes sought the Sword of Sapentia as it rested just inches beyond King Malif's reach.

"You should have been satisfied with the *first* deal," the king said, smiling through his crooked teeth. "But then again, I wouldn't have had the pleasure of executing you with your own magic blade."

Pressing the razor-sharp edge of his own sword against Lukas's neck, Malif slowly set the Shield of Aequant aside and snatched the Sword of Sapentia from the floor.

Cling!

Clang!

Clung!

Three blades suddenly dropped to the marble floor — Malif's black sword, the silver Sword of Sapentia, and a new broadsword — broken, crooked, bent, and blacker than the first.

Climbing to his feet Lukas tossed the new sword aside as he recalled the words of Lord Custor of Sapentia: *If the impure and foolish take hold of the Sword of Sapentia to claim it as their own, they will be turned into blades of falsehood.* He snatched the Sword of Sapentia from the floor, replaced the Helmet of Validaan on his head and, his heart pounding with excitement, lifted the Shield of Aequant with his left hand.

Gazing upon the rear wall, Lukas read the covenant engraved on the foundation of the great spire. The time had come to enforce it.

Chapter Seven

The Cavern of Flames

I

When the people heard that the man of Addis's vision had arrived in Lexor to confront the king, their hearts were ignited by a new hope. So shortly after Lukas entered the palace of King Malif a throng of peasants began gathering outside the castle gate. Dozens of soldiers assembled at the palace to keep order, but they had never seen the people so stirred with excitement. The soldiers knew that if the unrest turned to violence, their greatest efforts would be unable to extinguish the flames of rebellion that burned in the people's hearts.

When Lukas finally emerged from the palace gate, silence quickly fell over the masses. All eyes and ears turned to Lukas, and though he had not planned a speech, he knew they expected him to say something. "People of Lexor," he began, "today King Malif's unlawful reign has come to an end. I have seen the forgotten covenant engraved on the wall of the throne room, and I am determined to see the promise remembered and fulfilled."

Lukas did not need any more words. The crowd applauded, old men and women wept with joy, and little children danced, though they were not sure why. Only the soldiers received the words with anxiety, backing away from the cheering crowd uneasily. When Lukas saw the fear on the soldiers' faces, he recognized that the tension must be relieved before something terrible happened.

After quieting the crowd Lukas turned and addressed the soldiers in a strong voice, loud enough for all to hear, "Protectors of Lexor, I know your service to King Malif was forced just like the slave labor of the people. With the end of Malif's reign you have been relieved of your duties. However order must still be maintained. Your service to the *people* of Lexor is needed now *if* you are willing."

The soldiers froze, looking at each other for direction. Lukas had suddenly opened a way of escape for them, but they were not sure if they should or could take it. Were they still loyal to the vanquished King Malif? Because the king had no heir, was anybody among them capable of giving orders? All eyes fell on the ranking soldier, Sergeant Doro, who had escorted Lukas into the palace.

Doro stepped forward and slowly drew his sword. Uneasy gasps bubbled from the crowd, but rather than attacking the old soldier turned his blade around and carefully handed it to Lukas. "On behalf of the soldiers," he said, "I accept this new responsibility in the service of the people if *they* are willing."

The crowd of commoners nodded and mumbled their consent as the tension between the soldiers and the people eased. When the soldiers took their place among the people, Addis stepped out of the crowd. He and Doro exchanged familiar glances, and the sergeant bowed slightly before the man he had recently derided as a slave. In an unexpected gesture Addis approached the old sergeant and clasp his shoulder. Leaning forward Addis whispered something in Doro's ear — a secret message between two old friends once estranged, but now reconciled. When tears filled Doro's eyes, Addis turned from the crowd and approached Lukas.

"My lord," he began. The crowd hushed at the voice of their beloved sage. "May we see the covenant for ourselves?"

Lukas smiled at the sudden formality of his otherwise familiar guide. "Of course, by rights the palace is yours."

Lukas led the people in a great procession through the outer wall. The mood of the crowd shifted from excitement to awe as they slowly filed through the beautiful garden, up the cascading steps, along the marble hall, and into the luxurious throne room – a sight no peasant of Lexor had ever seen.

Pointing to the statues of soldiers spread throughout the room, some of the people of Lexor mumbled that "the wretched decorations have to go." Others wondered, *What kind of king would display such violent pieces of art and so poorly placed?* Lukas smiled at the comments and laughed out loud when a little child picked up the sword that had once been King Malif and began swinging it around like a toy, only to be scolded by his mother.

As Lukas and Addis stood amidst the shuffling citizens staring at the message engraved in bold letters on the eastern wall, the elder raised his brows. "You'll have to tell me all about the battle."

"It was . . . interesting."

"You know they'll want to make you king," Addis whispered.

Lukas frowned. "I suppose they will. After two generations of evil tyranny most expect me to be just a nicer tyrant. You know, of course, I would never accept such a position."

Addis nodded. "They *will* need some sort of government."

"I've been thinking about that very problem, and something tells me you have, too . . . for many years. You're their natural leader, Addis. They may fear and respect me, but they honor and trust you as I do." Lukas turned to his new friend and continued, "I only wish I could stay longer."

"You finally decided which direction on the compass to follow?" Addis asked with just a touch of humor.

"West," Lukas replied, "back to Mount Timor."

II

"Lukas, stop fighting!" his mother screamed. "You must save Lilia!"

Lukas stood in the center of a large hallway holding the sword and shield while his mother and father called to him from a safe place farther down the hall. While dancing flames closed in on him, Lukas saw Lilia just a few feet away shrouded in smoke. As he attempted to reach through the smoke to rescue her, a wall of flame burst from the floor and blocked his way.

Lilia screamed. Lukas stepped forward into the flame as the sword and shield began to melt. When he reached the other side, his clothes were burning. Lilia cowered in fear as Lukas found himself engulfed in flames. She backed away from his fiery grip, and Lukas fell.

Covered in flames Lukas dropped through darkness like a falling star plummeting from heaven. . . . He landed on a hard bed in the palace of Lexor. Sitting up, he opened his eyes and saw the bright flame of a candle just a foot from his face. A gentle hand had shaken him awake. Without thinking Lukas blurted out his friend's name: "Taro?"

"No, it's Addis."

Lukas lay back in the bed and covered his eyes with his hand. "Could you put the fire out?"

Addis paused and glanced at the candle. "No," he answered, "*you* put it out."

Lukas sat up on the side of the bed and stared at the candle flickering in the darkness, highlighting Addis's face and beard with an orange glow. He leaned forward to blow, but Addis pulled the candle away. "No, use your fingers. The pain will be brief."

Lukas understood; it was a test.

He wet his fingers and slowly reached out his right hand to squeeze the burning wick. Though he had traveled hundreds of miles into unknown and dangerous lands, those three inches to the flickering flame were the most difficult. Drawing on every ounce of strength and will he possessed he smothered the candlelight, leaving behind a trail of wax-scented smoke.

Addis tossed the candle aside. "Well done, my lord. Now let me tell you what I saw this morning in my dream."

Lukas listened attentively.

"You will face the dragon, Haarlok, not many days from now. You will slay her . . ."

"And Lilia?" Lukas interrupted.

"She's alive," Addis said excitedly. "You'll see her soon, and she will escape."

Lukas's heart began to race but not with fear. Hope reignited in his soul, and he immediately stood and started dressing for his journey.

"The dream included much more," Addis added quickly, "but I don't have time to tell you now. The fastest horses in Lexor are waiting for us outside. Everything has been arranged. We need to leave immediately."

Lukas glanced up from gathering his things and said, "*We?*"

"Did you think I would leave you when the journey has just begun? The elders have been appointed . . ."

"The people need you, Addis," Lukas interrupted. "You *have* to stay."

With a sigh Addis confessed: "*I* was in the dream too, Lukas. I saw myself standing there before the fiery gate of Haarlok's lair. I learned decades ago that my visions cannot be changed. I must travel with you. Lexor will be waiting for me when I return."

III

Lukas squinted and rubbed sand from his sore eyes. Though the trip across the desert to Lexor had taken two days on foot, this morning they had crossed the bridge before noon and expected to reach Mount Timor by twilight. Lukas had never ridden such powerful horses. The water of Validaan they had drunk had obviously imparted incomparable speed and endurance.

"Where is that smoke coming from?" Lukas asked. He pointed to a plume of gray smoke rising beyond the Trembling Mountains.

"I'm not sure," Addis said, "but it's far beyond Timor. We must stay focused."

The shaft of smoke continued to trouble Lukas as he drank from his silver flask. "It must be the army of Trallia. The battle with Haarlok has begun."

"All the more reason to ride!" Addis exclaimed, kicking at his black stallion and galloping north toward Timor.

Lukas hesitated, staring at the column of smoke. Whatever was happening north of the mountains he was too far away to help. He had to retrieve the Armor of Fortis as quickly as possible.

The two riders traveled north for a short distance and then turned west along the road Lukas had followed from the Trembling

Mountains days earlier. Several long hours later, as the sun began to set below the jagged mountain ridge, both men's eyes grew heavy and their weary bodies slumped lower and lower. While they drifted in and out of sleep, their horses meandered up a steep incline.

"You have come back!" barked a deep voice.

Lukas's eyes shot open, and he nearly fell off his horse while Addis casually turned his attention to a stout dwarf smoking a pipe on the side of the road.

Pointing at Addis, Kraag squinted at Lukas and jibed, "And I see you brought your grandpa to help."

Lukas dismounted quickly as Addis eased himself from his mount.

"This is Addis of Lexor," Lukas announced, "my guide . . . and friend."

Kraag lifted his thick brows in surprise. "Did you say Lexor? *No one* is from Lexor. How'd you get here?"

Addis smiled and pointed at their rides, "By horse."

The dwarf mumbled something under his breath, cleared his throat, and spoke to Lukas: "You already tried to conquer the Tunnels of Timor, lad. And it's too late to let you in tonight. It would be past midnight before I rescued you from the top, and all my helpers went to bed hours ago." He took another puff of his pipe. "Come back in the morning."

"Open the door for him, little friend," Addis said calmly, "and then go to bed. If he does not make it to the other end within the hour, I will drag him down myself."

The dwarf shook his head slowly at first, chewed on his pipe for a moment, and sighed. "Very well," he conceded, reaching to his side and fiddling with a set of keys, "follow me."

The dwarf led them several meters down the road to the main entrance. With a rapid twist of his wrist he unlocked the massive door.

Lukas stepped forward, secured his belongings, and turned to say farewell to Addis.

"I hope to see you soon," Lukas said to Addis. He handed him the flask of Validaan. "Take this just in case I don't return."

Addis pushed the flask away. "No, I'll be waiting for you on the other side of the mountain with the horses. We'll drink there."

With that Lukas entered the darkness of the Tunnels of Timor for the second time and began descending the stairs as the metal door crashed behind him with a dark finality.

IV

Lukas raced down the rusty spiral staircase, skipping steps to reach the bottom. Ignoring the first silver ladder he swung open the door to the dark cavern and charged into the room, drawing his sword and holding the Shield of Aequant in front of him. As he ran, a faint yellow glow emanated from the shield providing a shallow beacon of light to guide his way. He leaped over rocks and dodged pits of murky water. Just beyond the light he could see the eyes of several creatures shifting and moving in the dark.

Suddenly one of the creatures jumped from the darkness into the glow of his shield. Lukas swung the Sword of Sapentia before he could even see what kind of beast had attacked him. With great force he struck one of its flailing limbs. When it turned to stone and fell to the ground, Lukas glanced at it — a white, hairless spider about the size of a wolf with large wings and sharp fangs. Though it alarmed him, he continued through the cavern without stopping. He sliced at two more of the giant insects before reaching the other end.

Within a minute Lukas found the entrance to the twisting tunnel that led to the windy canyon. He stopped, secured the shield firmly to his belt, tightened the strap on the helmet, and then pulled open the metal door.

Without delay he sprang from the stone landing and plummeted into the ravine. Just as before, the invisible grip of the violent winds snatched Lukas from his fall, carrying him into the heights of the canyon, and hurling him onto the other side where he landed firmly on his own feet.

"The sword!" he cried. The weapon had been ripped from his hilt during his flight. He turned toward the canyon and saw the

Sword of Sapentia spinning wildly in the air. Caught by a gust of wind, it lingered for a moment about a hundred feet above the bridge, then suddenly spun in a circle and darted toward him like an arrow launched from a bow. Stepping quickly to the side he snatched the sword from the air and sheathed it in one quick motion.

After a deep breath Lukas followed the contours of the narrow tunnel leading to the dreaded cavern of flames. He began to feel warm as he approached the red light seeping through the window on the steel door. He eyed the rungs of the third silver ladder on his right and the pain of his failure felt like a blade piercing his chest. Turning away from the ladder he focused all his attention on the door and tightened his grip on the Shield of Aequant.

Swallowing hard, Lukas opened the metal door with a quick tug.

An explosion rocked the cavern and blasted the door wide open. The shock hurled Lukas to the floor of the anteroom, knocking him unconscious.

A moment later Lukas opened his eyes, his face covered with black soot. The door was wide open and lava flowed toward him. A red blaze of flames followed and forced him to stand while a whirlwind of flame sprang up and blocked both exits. Lukas panicked, leaped to the rungs of the silver ladder, and hoped with all his might that the fire would retreat. Instead it swelled, intent on destroying the young intruder.

As flames began to burn his feet, Lukas screamed in pain and fear. He lost all his senses and reached for the escape hatch which moaned when he opened it. In utter panic, Lukas climbed up the dark shaft while the fire followed, nipping at his heels. Just in time, he sprang from the top of the mountain and rolled away from the fire shooting through the tunnel like a cannon blast.

Out of breath, Lukas opened his eyes and saw Addis and Kraag staring down at him. Addis shook his head. "I was afraid that you wouldn't make it. *Now* what will I tell the people of Lexor . . . their deliverer is a coward?"

The dwarf just laughed and puffed on his pipe. "What a waste of time! I'm going to bed! You're worse than the rest . . . at least *they* knew when to quit!"

Suddenly another man appeared. King Lundin stepped into view with a scowl on his face. "You were our only hope. I should never have given you that map!"

Then Lilia appeared too, her white dress torn, her ash-covered face marked by the tears running down her cheeks. "I was waiting for you," she cried, "but you never came." Without warning the earth shook and fire burst upon the mountain top. In the dark sky Lukas saw a massive yellow serpent slithering to and fro spewing fire as it writhed. A second later Haarlok swooped down and snatched the others, leaving Lukas alone on the mountain. Closing his eyes he screamed in agony though his body felt no pain.

V

Lukas awoke with a start, his own scream echoing through the dark tunnels. He was lying on his back in the anteroom before the door to the cavern of flames. Realizing he had been caught in a dream he jumped to his feet with the images of all four faces firmly etched in his mind.

Overcome by a sense of relief he looked through the window into the fiery cave. A new resolve welled up in his heart. For once in his life, his mind, emotions, and will were one, and no fear, however great, would stop him.

He opened the door carefully and stepped in. Behind him the door slammed shut and locked leaving no opportunity for retreat. He was going through the cavern of flames even if it meant his doom.

Lukas scanned the chamber in search of the safest route. The cavern appeared calm though he knew it could erupt again at any moment. Pools of molten rock overflowed, flames waltzed across the surface of the lava, and black smoke clouded everything. He examined the path winding through the cave toward the exit. Though it would take longer than cutting straight across, he chose to stay on the intended trail rather than forge his own path.

With his first step the cavern began to tremble. His heart

pounded and sweat ran into his eyes as he held the Shield of Aequant firmly to protect himself from any sudden explosions. A pool of lava erupted in the far corner, and molten rock spattered the walls and ceiling, but nothing touched him.

Suddenly a small fire ignited on the path in front of him. He stepped back, and another started burning behind him. Though he kicked at the fire, it merely grew until it was half his height, licking the silver shield with tongues of flame.

Standing between the pillars of fire frantically searching for a solution, Lukas instantly realized the obvious. An endless supply of water was hanging from his belt! Until now his reason had been so blinded by fear that he had not thought of the magic silver flask!

Snatching the flask of Validaan and twisting off its cap, he poured the water on the path and the flames were instantly extinguished. Steam billowed from the hot ground as more water flowed onto the path and gathered into a long stream. The narrow walkway through the cavern had been carved into the stone floor, and it sloped in a gradual decline, allowing the water to run through the shallow trench for several feet in front of him. The water hissed, boiled, and evaporated as it ran along the trail, and all the way along the path the fire was quenched.

Picking up his pace, Lukas soon found himself in the center of the cavern. A tremor thundered through the mountain and rocks dropped from the ceiling, splashing into a nearby pool of exploding lava. Lukas would have been badly burned had he not held the silver shield in front of him to deflect the blast. Hot chunks of rock bounced off his helmet, but still the water flowed.

The path twisted around a corner to the right and then cut to the left before abruptly crossing a narrow river of molten rock. Lukas crossed the river in two quick steps. The cavern shook again almost as if it were making a last attempt to destroy its intruder before he reached the exit just a few feet away.

In disbelief Lukas opened the door and stepped out of the cavern of flames.

When the door closed behind him, Lukas found himself standing silently in a round, marble room just the size of his bedchamber back home. The cool room was lit by several round windows through which the light from the chamber of fire spilled, illuminating a silver breastplate and chain mail resting atop a steel armor stand.

In the center of the breastplate the ancient seal of the House of Stanton glistened — a golden eagle wearing a helmet with a sword and shield in its claws. Childhood memories of that same seal flashed through his mind. It had adorned the display armor of Stanton, the walls and doors of his family's estate, the wax seal on every letter, and even the embroidery on his parents' clothes. It harkened back to an age when the House of Stanton — not the House of Lundin — ruled over Trallia. With tears in his eyes Lukas reached out and touched his family seal.

Chapter Eight

The Fiery Gate

I

When Lukas donned the chain mail and breastplate, he experienced no sudden transformation, no burst of power, or surge of magic. Instead he felt uncomfortable, overburdened, and clumsy. Yet those thoughts left him as his attention turned to a small square of parchment attached to the empty stand, the fourth and final segment of the ancient map. Lukas held all four pieces in his hands and examined the complete map in the flickering light before placing them all in his pocket.

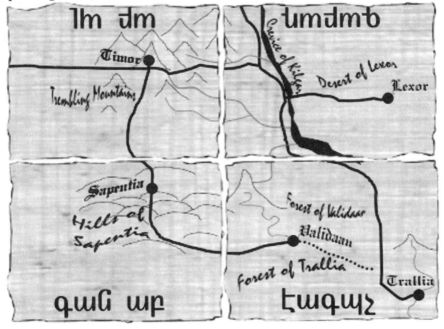

Eager to flee his underground nightmare, Lukas left through the door on the opposite end of the marble chamber. He quickly realized that the exit from Mount Timor was designed to prevent anybody from snatching the Armor of Fortis without passing through the three trials. To that end, two more one-way doors separated him from the outside world.

When Lukas emerged from Mount Timor he saw Addis standing in the silver light of the moon holding the reins of their horses and grinning proudly. Kraag had ridden Lukas's steed around the mountain to see if, in fact, the lad would make it. When the door opened, the dwarf fell off his horse and dropped his pipe into a deep ravine.

Without a word to either of them, Lukas marched forward, the Armor of Fortis clanking at each step. He immediately embraced Addis who sighed loud enough to cause the horses to stir.

"Unbelievable," Kraag said, fidgeting with his beard.

Lukas slowly removed the four map fragments and handed them to Addis who pointed at a small oil lantern sitting on the ground. "Can you lift that for me?" the old sage asked.

With no fear of the flame Lukas lifted the lantern and held its flickering light close enough for Addis to read the map. Kraag tried to stand on his toes to look on as well, and Addis graciously squatted to accommodate the little man's stature.

After carefully examining the four fragments Addis looked up at Lukas and announced, "The message says, *kogah ba nag, lo ba dabag.*"

The dwarf translated his own language: "Strength is in attaining, not in possessing."

Lukas frowned. "What does it mean?"

The three men glanced at each other. "It means," Addis finally said, standing up and heading for his horse, "that we'll know what it means when we discover its meaning."

The dwarf eyed Addis skeptically. "Spoken like a true wise man . . . who knows nothing of Dwarfish lore." Turning to Lukas he explained, "No, lad, the message is an old proverb. It means your strength is not found in what you carry on the outside, but in what you are on the inside."

"I still don't understand," Lukas said.

Addis shook his head. "Forget it. Dwarves can mine proverbs for meaning better than they can mine mountains for gold."

Kraag ignored the comment and answered, "The proverb means that your quest has changed you, made you more real than you were before. We like to say: *Fa saa borin'taan, e na ba laan; da pra' mori raan, ou da rabaan* . . . As rock mined from the ground and refined in the fire; the end is more real than the beginning." The dwarf knotted his thick brow. "Of course, it sounds much better in Dwarfish . . ."

Addis rolled his eyes and climbed onto his horse as Lukas removed the breastplate and chain mail, attaching them to the rear of his saddle. When Lukas mounted his ride, Addis said to the dwarf, "An interesting interpretation, my little friend."

Kraag frowned and mumbled something inaudible through his thick mustache. "Are you headed for home, lad?" he asked.

"No," Lukas answered, spurring his horse onto the mountain pass. "We are traveling north."

"To the lair of Haarlok," Addis clarified, looking down at the dwarf as he followed behind Lukas.

"Farewell, my friend," Lukas called. "If our quest is successful, we will meet again."

The dwarf shook his head in wonder as he watched the two men trot into the darkness. "Unbelievable," he said, and then began searching for his pipe.

Lukas and Addis rode several miles before setting up camp on the side of the road. They watered their horses at a nearby stream as they built a makeshift tent to shield them from the cool breeze blowing in from the north.

"Tomorrow we'll ride several hours to the north-south road," Addis said. "From there the dragon's lair is about seven more hours' ride on horseback. We'll arrive sometime in the evening, barring any delay."

Lukas secured the sword, helmet, shield, and armor beneath his saddle which sat in the tent just inches from his reach. Using his saddlebag as a pillow, he lay on his back and began to doze even as Addis continued to speak.

"The dwarf was probably right, you know," Addis mused, lying down on the ground. "The power of those weapons is something you achieve, not something to be possessed."

Lukas nodded as he drifted deeper into sleep.

"Like gold refined in fire you're more real now than you have ever been."

Lukas agreed with a short moan.

"And because you have changed," Addis concluded, "so has your world . . . and everything in it."

"Great," Lukas agreed, rolling onto his side and mumbling: "Now go to sleep, my friend."

II

In every tongue the mountain was called "Saalan," though its name originally came from the ancient Dwarfish words for "fire" and "rock." The volcano had been active for a thousand years, but nobody ever remembered it actually erupting. Some said the dragon Haarlok herself controlled the volcano from within, and if she traveled too far or too often they feared the mountain would explode.

Its main crater churned and boiled tossing hot ash or molten sludge into the air often enough for travelers to keep their distance — as if any would dare approach the legendary home of Haarlok. The crater was her main entrance and exit. She had even been seen on several occasions diving into its red hot magma, and ancient Dwarfish archives written by those who originally mined the volcano suggested the dragon would reemerge in a massive chamber within, high enough above the level of the lava to keep her victims alive. The truth was, however, that no one knew exactly what she did with her victims once they were taken into the heart of Saalan.

Besides the crater only one other possible entrance had been recorded in the Dwarfish histories. Long before Haarlok took up residence in Saalan dwarf miners had excavated a narrow tunnel from the southern base of the mountain up into a massive room from which diamonds had been mined until lava from the crater destroyed the entrance. Many suspected that Haarlok lived in that chamber feeding off the diamonds and molten lava as dragons do.

For the last five centuries the mine entrance had been covered by a constant wall of lava pouring from an opening above, dropping over the passage, and flowing into a pool that drained into the earth. Of course, no one in their right mind would have chosen to enter the dragon's lair through the mine entrance, and those few madmen who tried were incinerated as soon as they touched the fresh cascade of molten rock.

On their journey north into the region of the dragon Addis relayed these details about what lay ahead. When Lukas asked him where he had learned all this, Addis replied, "Oh, from a very old friend who knew such things," and continued on.

Lukas stirred uncomfortably on his horse, trying to imagine what sort of unexpected challenges he would face.

"I suspect," Addis said, "that whoever wears the helmet and armor will be able to pass through the fiery gate unharmed."

"You *suspect?*" Lukas moaned.

By mid-afternoon the two men passed through a narrow, shadowy gorge between two cliffs where the ground had recently been trampled by horses and men.

Lukas said, "The army of Trallia traveled through here."

Addis nodded. "These tracks head only north. They never returned."

Lukas swallowed hard and continued to ride.

An hour later the low road began to ascend a steep rocky incline where no plants or trees grew. The rocks and sand were black, and a thin layer of volcanic ash covered the earth. As they neared the top of the hill, Addis took the lead and turned around in his saddle. "Lukas, between this ridge and the Saalan is a great plateau. It's the only place the army of Trallia could have assembled." Addis's expression looked grim.

Lukas pulled his horse to a stop and listened carefully. He heard only his own breath, an occasional gust of wind across the rocks, and the shifting of the horses. Addis and Lukas stared at each other for at least a minute as they both listened attentively hoping to hear more than just silence.

Reluctantly Addis spoke: "Either the Trallian army is more silent than the whispering wind . . . or the Trallian army is no more."

III

The thin layer of gray ash that had covered the hill below lay thick on the vast plateau. As Lukas and Addis surveyed the gravelly plane by foot, the stench confirmed what they had suspected: the army of Trallia had been reduced to ashes. A random sword, bow, or article of armor could be seen protruding from the countless piles of dust, but otherwise there was nothing left to bury. In a few days whatever remains were left of the soldiers of Trallia would be swept away with the wind.

In the distance, perhaps a mile or more beyond, the Saalan smoldered silently, warning trespassers to stay away or suffer the same fate as the rest.

"King Stefan was right," Lukas said.

Addis looked at him, confused. "Right about what?"

"He feared his successors would destroy his kingdom," Lukas answered, recalling the words of the knight commander, Warrick. "It looks like King Lundin has succeeded in fulfilling the prophecy."

"How many men were in this army?" Addis asked, nudging aside a shield that had been twisted in the heat.

"Over four thousand," Lukas answered quietly.

Addis closed his eyes, not sure if he should feel despair or rage. Lukas simply stared at the volcano, squinting to keep the ash from burning his eyes.

"Let's ride," Lukas said, turning back toward his horse. "Maybe we can find the miner's tunnel before the sun sets."

Addis glanced at the sun which hovered low on the red horizon. They had less than an hour of light left. "If the entrance is really blocked by a fiery gate," Addis said, "then the light won't matter, will it? In fact it will be easier to find lava in the dark."

Lukas and Addis agreed to camp on the plateau and rest until midnight. Though they did not sleep, they were able to gather their wits and rest their weary limbs. When the stars shined brightly in the heavenly sphere, they remounted their horses and rode across the plateau toward the deep red glow of Saalan. They were concealed by the darkness in case the dragon happened to be watching for survivors.

Sometime after midnight Addis and Lukas came upon the fiery gate at the southern base of the mountain exactly where they expected it to be. As they approached, the horses whickered nervously, for the sight was worse than Lukas could have imagined.

Had it been cool and blue rather than hot and red, the gate could have been mistaken for a waterfall flowing down the side of the mountain. The lava fell about three stories from a five-foot-wide crack in the mountainside. On the ground it flowed to the left and right of a path that appeared to pass through the magma which swirled in two pools before draining into the depths of the earth. They could not be certain if the path guarded by the wall of molten rock actually led anywhere or not as the lava could just as easily have concealed a solid wall. Yet the Dwarfish legends had been accurate to this point, and ultimately Addis and Lukas had no other options.

The two men dismounted and unloaded their belongings. They drank from the water of Validaan and ate a few bits of hard bread from the provisions they had carried from Lexor. After Addis whispered something to the horses, they causally trotted away from the two pools of lava and rested quietly in the distance.

Setting the silver flask on the ground, Lukas donned the chain mail. It covered his body from his head to his feet. He then lifted the breastplate and attempted to place it on his chest. "Could you help me with this?" he asked Addis who was rummaging through his saddlebag.

Addis looked up. "Shouldn't we wait until morning?"

Lukas looked at the mountain and shook his head. "No," he said. "It took me two weeks to get this far. I'm going in now."

Addis stood and helped Lukas clasp the Armor of Fortis around his chest. It gleamed in the red glow of the lava though the instant he put it on his body felt cool. He placed the Helmet of Validaan on his head and secured the strap. Then after grabbing the Shield of Aequant in his left hand and the Sword of Sapentia in his right, he turned toward the fiery gate and stared for a moment, breathing deeply to calm his mind and heart.

With an indescribable sense of peace Lukas approached the end of the path and stood just a foot from the lava fall. The heat radiated on his face, but his helmet, armor, and shield seemed to protect him. Taking a deep breath Lukas pushed the tip of the Sword of Sapentia into the cascading magma.

Though it stayed cool, the sword shimmered, smoked, and melted away.

IV

"Stop!" Addis cried. He stared into a shallow pool of water that had spilled from the flask.

As he said this, Lukas staggered backward nearly tripping on the chain mail armor that hung down to his heels. "The sword! It's . . . gone!"

"Look!" Addis exclaimed, signaling for him to hurry.

Lukas, still shocked at the sudden loss of the sword, rushed noisily to Addis's side and stared into the pool of water. Though his mind still lingered on the sword, his eyes immediately widened as he saw a vision reflected on the surface of the magic waters of Validaan, like the mystical visions he had seen in the Garden itself. The waters revealed Lukas standing in a cave dressed only in his green tunic and covering his face with his arms as his entire body was engulfed by Haarlok's fiery breath. The vision dissolved and another scene replaced it. Addis and Lilia rode across the plane on a single horse as the sun rose on the horizon. Then the vision in the waters faded away.

As the waters of the pool slowly began to boil and steam, Addis continued to stare at it and whispered, "Lukas, I didn't share a part of my dream with you. I wasn't going to because I didn't understand it."

"Go on," Lukas urged.

Addis pointed into the pool where the vision had just faded. "That was my dream. You were consumed by Haarlok's fire. Yet somehow you slay the dragon, and Lilia escapes. I can't see the whole picture; I don't know how the pieces fit together." He gave Lukas a blank stare: "You'll be burned alive in there."

Lukas bit his lip anxiously and thought about this for a long time. Suddenly a sense of peace replaced his anxiety, and he stared at his old friend. "Addis, in your dreams do you see what *might* be or what *will* be?"

Addis shook his head. "I see only the future, the future that can never change."

Lukas closed his eyes. He imagined Lilia in the mountain just a few yards away. If Addis's dreams could be trusted, she was alive but despairing of life. He opened his eyes and looked at his empty hand where the Sword of Sapentia had dissolved in his grasp. "Strength is in attaining, not in possessing," he whispered to himself. Nodding in understanding and resolve, Lukas placed his hand on Addis's shoulder and said, "Take good care of her, my friend."

With those final words Lukas turned and burst through the fiery gate.

Chapter Nine

The Lair of Haarlok

Though his eyes were closed tight and his face turned down, he knew the shield began to vaporize the moment it touched the lava fall. The helmet that protected his head and the armor that guarded his body endured longer than the shield, but they too gradually faltered as Lukas's body went from cool to hot in seconds.

The flow of molten rock was heavier than he expected, and he had to muster all his strength to keep from collapsing under its tremendous weight. As his legs trembled and his feet began to burn, he pressed through the plunging magma into open air where he could finally breathe again. With his eyes closed as tightly as possible for fear that the hot air and gases would still blind him, Lukas dropped to a hot stone floor, rolled onto his back, and kicked off his smoldering leather shoes.

The sword, shield, helmet, and armor he had strived to obtain had been lost in a matter of minutes, but he had made it through the fiery gate. *Strength is in attaining, not in the possessing,* he thought to himself. He was desperate to believe those words. At the same time he recalled the vision in the water and Addis's dream that he would be burned alive in the dragon's lair. With his eyes still closed Lukas lay on his back considering his next move and listened to his own breath for what seemed like several minutes.

While his breathing calmed, he noticed a hot draft of putrid air blowing gently over his face. Even though he kept his eyes shut, Lukas sensed a large, bright object moving above him like sunlight bursting through a break in the clouds. So strong was the brilliance that when Lukas gradually opened his eyes, he expected to see a mighty flame or perhaps the sun itself. Instead his vision was filled with the large, yellow face of Haarlok staring down at him through her six monstrous eyes.

Seven horns grew around the top of Haarlok's head like a crown, and at the center of her skull two spiraled horns twisted like those of a ram. Her six eyes glared balefully from her reptilian face in three pairs. The two eyes on the top looked almost human with deep black pupils and green irises. A pair of red serpentine slits sat in the middle, dilated wide in the dim light of her lair. The lower eyes were black, lidless disks like an insect that could see in the darkest places. Haarlok's large, snakelike mouth gaped with several sharp fangs glittering menacingly.

Lukas and the dragon stared at each other, and as the young man focused on the ancient beast's black, spider-like eyes he began to feel her whispering words running through his mind. Her eerie, hoarse voice sounded like an old woman murmuring softly while she inhaled, though the dragon's mouth did not move: "I am the fire . . . I am the light . . . I am the first . . . I am the last . . ."

Lukas realized the dragon was engaged in endless self-adoration and praise: "I am loved . . . I am hated . . . I am worshipped . . . I am feared . . ."

Lukas closed his eyes and the chanting faded. The bright outline of the dragon remained as if projected onto his mind. He heard his own heart beating in his chest, and he yearned desperately to fall through the darkness and land in his bed to scream out in fear and anguish rather than open his eyes and face the dragon's mesmerizing gaze.

Then his thoughts suddenly turned to Lilia. *She must be here somewhere,* he thought. At that moment the dragon's fiery image vanished and a mental picture of Lilia materialized in its place. *Does she know I'm here? Can she see me?* His heart raced faster but not with fear.

Lukas opened his eyes and the whispering began again: "I am near . . . I am far . . . I am everywhere . . . I am nowhere. . . ." He rolled onto his hands and knees and slowly pushed himself from the hot stone floor to stand unsteadily on his bare feet.

Glancing quickly at his surroundings, Lukas noticed a red glow emanating from the fiery gate behind him while another swirling pool of molten rock gave off a steady orange light in the distance.

"I am perfect . . . I am glorious . . ."

He looked around for Lilia but saw nothing. Most of the cave was hidden in dark corners and crevices, and he suspected she might be cowering in one of those. Besides that, the dragon's enormous serpentine body coiled throughout the lair, hiding most of the cave from his sight.

"I am beautiful . . . I am dreadful . . ."

Yes, thought Lukas, *you* are *dreadful.* He looked into her eyes again and the muttering grew louder.

"I am wonderful . . . I am terrible . . ."

"Yes," Lukas agreed, this time aloud, "you *are* wonderful and terrible."

At the sound of Lukas's words, Lilia's voice echoed from the shadows like the distant ringing of a silver bell: "Close your eyes or you'll start worshipping her yourself!"

II

When Lilia called out, Haarlok squirmed. For the first time since Lukas entered the lair, the dragon spoke with her mouth while the whispering continued in the background: "Do not listen to her!" she ordered. Her voice carried the authority of a queen though it hardly sounded human.

Lukas continued to stare into the dragon's eyes as if caught in her hypnotic gaze.

The whispers continued: "I am brilliant . . . I am vast . . ."

Lilia spoke again. "No! Whoever you are, listen to me! The whispering will stop if you close your eyes."

The dragon shuddered, and her upper eyes narrowed with anger. Lukas saw several of her many arms clawing at the ground in irritation.

"Lilia!" Lukas called out, "I've come for you!" His voice swelled with emotion when he realized she did not recognize him. Even though he had closed his eyes, he sensed fiery Haarlok slithering around in the cave.

Silence filled the room for a moment, and then Lilia spoke. "Lukas! I knew you would come!"

"Silence!" Haarlok shrieked. Lukas heard the dragon move quickly and saw her glowing form shifting before him. The dragon struck Lilia, who screamed in pain, and Lukas resisted the urge to open his eyes.

"Leave her alone!" Lukas shouted.

"Do not speak with her again," Haarlok advised, "or I will eat her alive while you watch!" Haarlok lowered her face just inches from his and covered him with her sulfuric breath. Then she asked slowly, "What is your name, boy?" She examined his ragged tunic, singed hair, and burnt feet.

Lukas hesitated, but his fear of losing Lilia to the dragon made him answer. "I am Lukas, son of Stanton."

The dragon suddenly shuddered, took a step backward, and exclaimed, "What! You are the son of the last lord and lady of the House of Stanton?"

Lukas's heart beat faster, and his warm skin broke into a cold sweat. His response faltered before the words would fall from his tongue: "No," he corrected. "I *am* the last lord of the House of Stanton."

The dragon laughed viciously before declaring, "I thought I had killed you with your parents years ago!"

Lukas's breathing stopped as the glowing figure of the beast moved closer. A thousand images of his nightmares flashed through his mind – the fire, the smoke, the burning halls, the horrified faces of his mother and father, the explosion, the fall. Suddenly they all dissolved into the flaming outline of the dragon. Still he kept his eyes closed.

Her laughter ceased, and she said calmly, "Now I will have the pleasure of destroying the House of Stanton *again*."

Trembling, Lukas opened his mouth and spoke the first words that came to him. "No," he said, "I have seen the future. Tonight you will be slain, and Lilia will go free."

The dragon laughed while all her claws scratched the stone floor like fingernails on a slate. "You are wrong, boy. Tonight I will destroy the Houses of Stanton and Lundin together! I expected that heartless King of Trallia to come for his daughter, but this is much better! At last I will repay the ancient heroes of Trallia for slaying my children and consorts for generations! Their noble lines will be reduced to ashes, and I will leave whatever is left of them to be blown away in the wind. King Stefan warned me long ago that a king of his line would slay me. Tonight his prophecy will be annulled!"

Like a venomous snake preparing to strike, Haarlok drew back, inhaled with a gasp, and blasted Lukas with a torrent of white fire that melted the rocks around him. The scene that had appeared in water and dreams was fulfilled in a moment while Lilia screamed in anguish and rage.

III

The inferno lasted for nearly a minute. When Haarlok stopped her fiery assault, silence filled the lair as Lilia sobbed noisily in the distance.

Haarlok stared at the place where Lukas once stood as a barefoot boy in a ragged, green tunic. That boy was gone forever, consumed by the dragon's breath.

In his place stood a tall, young man clothed in brilliant light. His head was covered with the Helmet of Validaan. In his left hand the Shield of Aequant shimmered with a faint, yellow glow and in his right the Sword of Sapentia radiated with brilliant light. The Armor of Fortis covered his body, and on his chest the seal of the House of Stanton pierced the darkness.

The dragon stared in shock at Lukas, and for the first time in centuries her whispering self-worship ceased.

She took a step back and blasted Lukas with another downpour of fire. The ceiling of the cave above Lukas turned red and dropped onto the cavern floor in large clumps. When she stopped, panting for air, Lukas still stood straight and strong, the silver armor shining brighter than before.

Haarlok cursed Lukas and spat another narrower shaft of fire at him, but this time Lukas raised the Sword of Sapentia and deflected the flames back at the dragon, burning her eyes. The fire ceased and the dragon writhed in pain, hurling a flood of curses instead of flames. She flopped around like a snake caught by its tail, rubbing her burning eyes on the ground.

As a thick cloud of smoke cleared away, Lukas looked up to see Lilia standing across the lair on a ledge, staring at him in disbelief. Black soot stained her tattered white dress, and her once beautiful hair hung down on her shoulders like moss on a rock. Though her eyes were red and swollen with tears, she refused to blink for fear that the luminous vision of Lukas would vanish.

Haarlok suddenly stopped moaning and cursing and turned back to Lukas. Without warning she lunged forward, raised her hands into the air, and slashed at him with her razor-sharp claws. But her claws passed through him as if he were made of light. She swung again but with no effect. She stopped and squinted at Lukas through her damaged eyes. In disbelief she stuttered, "You . . . you . . . are . . . not . . . real!"

Lukas recalled Kraag's proverb: *As rock mined from the ground and refined in the fire, the end is more real than the beginning.* "You are wrong," Lukas said, taking a bold step forward as the dragon cowered in fear, "The truth is *I* am now more real than *you.*"

He raised his blade and swung it at the dragon which recoiled instantly. In a sudden fit of desperate rage she sprang at him with all her might. After her body passed through Lukas like a ghost, Haarlok slammed through the outer wall of the cave and burst into the starry night. For the first time in eons fresh air flowed into Haarlok's lair as the dragon collapsed onto the outside ground, unconscious, and half-buried beneath rock and lava.

IV

The armor and weapons of light had already begun to fade away as Lukas leapt over stones and debris to reach Lilia. She rushed toward him, and they embraced. He held her like he would never let her go.

"I came for you," he sobbed. "I failed in Trallia! I ran when the dragon attacked! But I came for you!"

"Through fire and flame," Lilia said, overwhelmed with emotion.

A moment later, Lukas removed the silver-chained necklace from his vest pocket and reached over Lilia's shoulders to clasp the red amulet around her neck.

Shaking with nervousness, Lukas once again struggled to attach the silver chain. As the shaking grew, he realized that more that just his hands were trembling. A deep rumbling moved throughout his body, and soon everything around him was shuddering. The necklace dropped to the stone floor of the cave but Lukas quickly retrieved it. He and Lilia turned to see that Haarlok had begun to stir, shaking dirt and rock from her long, yellow body and waking from her stupor.

"Lukas, get out of there!" Addis shouted. Through a thin screen of smoke at the opening of the cave, Lukas could see Addis sitting on his horse, ready to ride.

"Let's go!" Lilia shouted. The lair continued to shake as the dragon slithered out from under the pile of debris.

Lukas hastily snatched the silver amulet from the ground and gently pulled Lilia to him. Just as the dragon turned its evil gaze toward them, Lukas carefully reached around Lilia's neck and finally attached the necklace with a click. He smiled at her, kissed her on her dry, cracked lips, then grabbed her hand and ran. They climbed a pile of rubble toward the exit as Haarlok sniffed the air and listened for signs of movement. Her vision had worsened when she crashed through the cavern, but she could sense that her prey was near.

Addis drew the dragon's attention by crying out and riding

noisily around Haarlok's tail. His horse leapt over the dragon's
spiked, yellow tail as she swiveled her head and shot a blast of fire
in his direction. But as quickly as he landed on the rocky ground,
Addis pulled the horse back and retreated again toward the high
pile of rocks where Lukas and Lilia were trying to climb down to
safety.

While the dragon angrily blasted fire in the wrong direction,
Addis steered his horse to the edge of the mound. "Jump!" he
shouted to Lilia as he glanced over his shoulder at the dragon just
a few yards away.

Lukas kissed Lilia again before she dropped down onto the
back of Addis's mount. Without hesitation Addis kicked the stallion
and rode off into the darkness. As she held onto the old man, the
horse galloped away from Mount Saalan. Lilia looked back to watch
Lukas as he attempted to climb down from the open lair, his bare
feet burning on the hot rocks.

Haarlok, hearing the horse's pounding hoofs, turned her gaze
toward Addis and Lilia and reared back to blast them with fire.

Lukas acted quickly, leaping from the rocky ledge and
tumbling to the ground. In one move he rolled to his feet between
Haarlok and his friends just as the dragon unleashed her fiery
breath. Lukas raised his left arm to stop the fire and was instantly
engulfed in flames.

Addis pulled his horse to a stop. He and Lilia watched from
afar as Lukas deflected Haarlok's fire, and the old seer squinted in
disbelief at what he saw — or thought he saw. Lukas stood his
ground completely clothed in the armor, helmet, and shield as the
fire reflected back at the dragon that was writhing in her own white-
hot fire.

A moment later the dragon exploded in a brilliant flash of
yellow and red fire that shot into the heavens and pierced the early
morning sky.

Chapter Ten

Return to Trallia

I

Once they were washed and rested the three companions headed south on the three-day journey home.

Addis rode his own horse just a few feet behind the couple and smiled every time Lukas whispered in Lilia's ear or pushed her hair from her soft cheek. Even when Lilia had emerged from the dragon's lair covered in soot, Addis sensed in her an inner beauty that mirrored Lukas's virtue. Now he regarded both of them with new eyes like those of a proud father watching a toddler take his first clumsy steps.

"Don't you two fall off that horse!" Addis called out when Lilia giggled so loudly at Lukas's words that it spooked the stallion into a brief gallop that ended with a sudden jolt.

Lukas turned back with a wide grin and saw that Addis had stopped. To his left the bridge across the Crevice of Kilgar stretched into Lexor, and Addis leisurely steered his horse to take it. Lukas whispered something in Lilia's ear and she nodded, turning her patient gaze toward Addis. Lukas then dropped down from his horse and reached into his saddlebag for the flask of Validaan. "I have a gift for you, my friend."

Addis watched him carefully. "What will you drink on the way home?" he asked.

"Lilia says there are rivers and streams all along this road to Trallia. We'll be fine."

Addis dismounted and embraced Lukas firmly.

Tears welled up in Lukas' eyes as he held the old man closely. "Thank you," he said, "for everything."

Addis stepped back and gave his young friend a puzzled look. "But it was *you* who rescued *me* from the side of the road just over there." He pointed to the place where Lukas had stopped to give him his first drink from the magic flask.

"I tried to walk past you," Lukas confessed.

Addis smiled. "*And* you saved Lexor from King Malif. Have you forgotten?"

"Of course not, but I can hardly take responsibility for that. You had to push me most of the way."

Addis shook his head. "You'll come around. You still think our paths crossed by accident, that all of this just fell into place. One day you'll discover something I learned long ago: you can take a thousand paths, but you can only go one way."

"So you've said," Lukas replied. The wry grin on his face belied that he knew the truth spoken by the old seer, and deep inside he hoped that one day he would have some of the wisdom of Addis.

Lukas took a deep breath, the kind a person takes to keep from breaking into tears. He handed Addis the flask with a nod. "Here, please take it. It's my gift of gratitude to you for helping me become a man."

The two friends embraced once again, and with a lump in his throat Addis said, "No farewells. I happen to know we'll see each other quite a bit in the future."

With a final wave Addis departed across the bridge to Lexor.

II

On the day Lilia had been snatched by Haarlok the palace grounds had been filled with thousands of people from the realm of Trallia, but the loss of human life had been minimal. It had always been told that Haarlok herself was tamer than either her husbands or children because she would rather abduct her victims than destroy them. Storytellers said that Haarlok relished the idea of being hunted by her victims' loved ones. It thrilled her to be pursued. But in truth those who lost family and friends to Haarlok's claws would have been better comforted by an outright slaying than capture. The victims were never rescued, and their unknown doom became an obsession for tormented imaginations.

In keeping with her pattern Haarlok spared most of the Trallians on the day she abducted the princess. However the castle of Trallia had suffered severe damage. The entire western tower had collapsed and lay in vast piles of rubble on the lawn. Most of the palace windows had been shattered, furniture and fixtures melted or burned, and huge sections of the exterior had crumbled. Black stains where soldiers had been incinerated still marred the beautiful marble of the garden courtyard just a few feet from where Lukas had proposed to Lilia. Besides the damage to the castle the nearest villages on the horizon beyond had been charred or flattened by wild fires sparked by the dragon's attack.

Returning home after three days' travel on horseback, Lukas and Lilia gasped when the castle came into view.

What alarmed them most was not the obvious physical damage to the palace and village but the disturbing silence. No visitors rode toward the castle, and no knight or soldier came forth to greet them. The posts of the watchmen stood empty, and the normal guards that patrolled the four roads leading to the castle were gone. Though a few black crows cawed and swooped down to the ground for food, no other sounds could be heard except the hoof beats of their own horse.

"Where is everyone?" Lilia asked nervously.

After departing Saalan Lukas had told Lilia of the army's decimation, but neither of them expected the desolation at home to be so severe.

"Is my father still alive?" she snapped. Unsure, Lukas could not answer. The couple quickly and quietly dismounted, allowing their horse to wander while they climbed a few steps to the courtyard. Lilia led the way. Crossing the place where they had stood before she had been snatched by Haarlok, Lilia passed through the open doorway leading to the king's public court.

When they saw that the castle appeared deserted, Lilia called out in a panic: "Hello! Is anybody here?"

Her voice reverberated in the large, marble audience chamber. Through a narrow doorway behind the king's empty throne a thud sounded as if someone had hit the floor with a mallet. "Who is there?" the king called.

Lilia's eyes lit up as she motioned for Lukas to follow, but he stopped and urged her on. "You go ahead. I'll join you in a moment."

Lukas lingered a few feet from the doorway and listened as Lilia rushed into a small, paneled room used for private audiences. Dark, parquet wood and a wide, red carpet covered the floor. Around the room the standards of the twelve families of Trallia decorated the walls. On the carpet halfway between the throne and the entrance, a large, golden apple still rocked back and forth after falling from the king's lap. Lilia saw him sitting on an old, wooden throne. When he saw his daughter burst through the open doorway, the king recoiled in horror, raising his forearms in front of his face as if afraid of losing his soul to a ghost.

"Father!" Lilia cried, ignoring his cowering. She rushed to him and embraced him. In shock the king slowly reached around and held her, unsure if he should trust his own senses.

"It *is* you, my daughter!" he finally cried. "It's really *you!*" King Lundin held his daughter like he would never let her go. "I thought I lost you!"

"No," Lilia said, kissing her stunned father on the cheeks and forehead.

"I thought Haarlok killed you just like she killed your mother!"

Lilia froze and slowly pushed herself away, breaking free from his magnetic embrace. She looked into his eyes and asked slowly, "What do you mean?"

The king's eyes turned to the floor, and he looked at the golden apple with great shame. He suddenly burst into tears and cried so loudly that it echoed all the way through the main audience hall and out to the courtyard.

Lilia stepped forward and held her father's frail hands. "Tell me, father," she said gently. "Please, tell me the truth."

III

"Your mother did not die in childbirth. Haarlok stole her just days after you were born."

Lilia sat on a padded stool beside her father's throne and stared into his blank face. King Lundin himself kept his eyes on the golden apple as he continued.

"From the day I assumed the throne of Trallia, I feared this evil most . . . that the dragon would come and destroy the House of Lundin as she had tried to do with Stanton. That's why the family of Lundin . . . not Stanton . . . rules over Trallia. They abdicated the throne a hundred years ago in fear of the dragon's wrath. My grandfather eagerly accepted the rule without regard for his own safety or that of his descendants."

The king stopped, realizing he had strayed a bit from his subject. He turned and looked into his daughter's tear-filled eyes. "Haarlok took your mother," he groaned. "She knew I would try to save her. And I *did* try . . . but I *failed.*"

With those words he pointed toward the golden apple lying on the floor. Lilia finally looked at it. "What is it?"

"That is an apple from the Golden Tree of Validaan," he explained, shaking his head. "I went to the Garden of Validaan to retrieve the first of four weapons needed to defeat Haarlok and rescue your mother. But I fell captive to the deception." The king began to weep uncontrollably. "I traded your mother for gold!"

Lilia wept out of pity for her father, wishing she could release him from his self-inflicted curse. "You *tried,*" she said, reaching out to embrace him.

"And *failed!*" he wept. "And now I've failed *again!*"

"But I've escaped," she answered, trying to inject hope into his fit of despair.

"But at what cost? Oh, my sweet Lilia, when you hear my other deeds you will never forgive me!"

She placed her hand on his shoulder, unsure if she was trying to steady herself or him, and asked slowly, "What did you do, father?"

"I sent the entire army to their destruction against the dragon! And . . . I sent Lukas on the quest I was unable to accomplish myself!" Lundin sobbed louder. "I sent Lukas to his death! I destroyed your kingdom and killed your groom! I don't deserve even your pity, much less your love!" Covering his face with trembling hands, the king buckled over in his throne.

"No, father, you're wrong!" Lilia exclaimed, leaping to her feet and prying his fingers from his wet face. "I *do* forgive you for your first mistake, but I cannot forgive you for killing Lukas. *Lukas is alive!*"

King Lundin suddenly looked up with bloodshot eyes as Lilia stepped aside and pointed toward the doorway. Lukas entered the chamber, took a few cautious steps along the red carpet, and stopped at the golden apple. The temptations of Validaan flashed through his mind for a moment before he casually kicked the golden apple into a corner. His eyes locked on the king's bewildered stare, and the two men regarded each other in silence.

Without a word, King Lundin rose from his throne, took two shaky steps toward Lukas, and threw his arms around him. "I cannot believe it! You . . . you *are* alive!"

Returning the embrace, Lukas said quietly, "I succeeded in the quest, my lord. I found the weapons . . . I slew the dragon . . . I returned with your daughter . . . just as I promised."

"I was wrong about you, Lukas. You are a far greater man than I will ever be." With those words, the king stepped back and removed the golden seal that hung from a silver chain around his neck. As Lilia began to weep, the king placed it over Lukas's shoulders with trembling hands. Lukas stared at the king in astonishment, his mind trying to come to terms with what his eyes had just witnessed. "I . . . I don't understand," he stuttered.

The king smiled for the first time in weeks and answered, "I only wish I had a greater kingdom to return to you, Lord of Stanton."

V

That evening, the first of his reign as King of Trallia, Lukas gathered together the small number of servants and soldiers who remained in the vicinity of the castle and began to restore what was left of the kingdom. However later that night Lundin pulled Lukas aside and led him down into the secret library where he had originally commissioned his quest. "I must share an important secret with you, my king. I can help you make your past a part of your future."

There in the silence of the library illuminated by a single candle, the former king of Trallia told Lukas the truth.

"It was fifteen years ago . . . on a summer night, shortly after midnight . . . when Haarlok struck," Lundin began solemnly as if he had rehearsed the words for years. "The vile serpent was bent on destroying the last members of the House of Stanton for good. Mad with rage she sought revenge against your father and mother, the last adult descendants of the family that once ruled over Trallia. Haarlok's spies had informed her that the Stantons were living in a large chateau in the southern foothills of Mount Trali. Day after day she watched to make sure your father hadn't acquired the sword and armor of King Stefan. At the right moment Haarlok struck with all her fury. Her goal that night was to leave no survivors. She knew that if the descendants of Stefan survived, it would one day be her doom."

Lukas could not speak. He stared at the candlelight as the story continued to unfold.

"By dawn the entire palace had been reduced to smoldering piles of charred wood and ash, and we could see a column of thick, black smoke for miles in every direction. My lookouts saw the smoke, and we knew something terrible had happened. I sent my palace guards under the command of Lord Karvon to render whatever aid was needed. As they neared the smoking ruins, Karvon recognized the carnage of Haarlok from afar and concluded that there could have been no survivors. But he followed his orders and combed the area anyway. To his astonishment, there was one survivor . . . you."

Lukas closed his eyes. Fiery images flashed through his mind. His mother crying out for his father to drop his sword . . . his father snatching Lukas away from the advancing flames . . . the family running through a large hall . . . an explosion . . . a scream . . . a fall.

Lukas opened his eyes and stared at Lundin who continued: "You had fallen through the burning floor and dropped to the lowest level of the chateau. Although you apparently tried to find your parents as the palace burned, you were trapped in a cellar when a rock wall collapsed and sealed you from the fire and heat. You waited there for two days before Karvon and his men arrived and prevented your stone refuge from becoming a tomb."

Lundin sighed. "I knew from the start why you feared fire, why you dreamed of smoke and flame. But I couldn't help you. I took you in as my ward, allowed you to dwell in the palace, commissioned Miss Poppit to raise you, and saw that Lord Karvon trained you as a warrior and nobleman alongside his son, Taro. But I deliberately taught you nothing of politics and the subtleties of aristocracy . . . partly to protect you but mostly to protect myself."

After a long silence Lundin said, "Forgive me for keeping you entombed in ignorance, for not granting you the honor of your family's legacy . . . for treating you like a helpless child rather than letting you become a real man."

VI

Governor Lundin observed the Spring Festival from his seat in the ballroom as the guests of Trallia sang, danced, and laughed in concert with the lively music. Both lords and commoners mingled on the palace grounds and the doors to the main ballroom stood open to allow people from the Kingdom of Trallia and their allies from the Republic of Lexor to come and go at will.

The Governor himself looked on with pride as his only daughter, Lilia, danced with his son-in-law, Lukas. On his right Miss Poppit held the Governor's first grandchild, Princess Sofi Lucia, named after her late maternal and paternal grandmothers. On the Governor's left the dark-skinned Addis stood tall, dressed in the long white robe of the Presiding Elder of Lexor. Despite their high ranks both men clapped along with the festive music.

King Lukas and Queen Lilia waltzed through the great ballroom doors out to the main garden courtyard, Lilia's delicate white dress waving at every turn. She had woven green ivy into her dark hair, matching the green tunic Lukas wore in the tradition of his native House of Stanton.

When the music ceased and the crowd cheered, Lukas held Lilia's hand high as she bowed gracefully. Lukas bowed as well, staring lovingly into Lilia's dark brown eyes. With his right hand he touched her smooth cheek, and Lilia's shy gaze retreated to the marble pavement.

King Lukas embraced his wife and kissed her gently. The vast throng cheered, and festive music burst forth echoing through the garden courts and beyond the palace grounds. A moment later the earth itself began to tremble . . . but this time it quaked with thunderous joy.